The Last Dance

May your heart sing!
♡ *Kiki Hamilton*

Kiki Hamilton

THE LAST DANCE

ISBN:1479391786

ISBN-13: 978-1479391783

Library of Congress Control Number:2012919664

CreateSpace Independent Publishing Platform
North Charleston, South Carolina

Fair Wind Books

First Printed in the United States of America

January 2013

Though this story and all of the characters are fictional, there are small portions inspired by my real life, thanks to the following:

Carly, Colin, Mitchell, Lilly, Keenan and Jordan – who can all dance to Michael Jackson's Thriller just as well as Mira. Love you guys.

Donna Russell, the real owner of Jefferson Christopher Beetle, who is not stick-shift challenged – here's to many fond memories of growing up together.

The real Dr. Murdoch, who helped us through some terrible times with her extraordinary medical knowledge and heartfelt support.

And to Fena Lee … my charming and witty friend in Singapore, who taught both me, and Mira, a new way to swear. ☺

Also by Kiki Hamilton

THE FAERIE RING
(Book One of The Faerie Ring Series)

THE TORN WING
(Book Two of The Faerie Ring Series)

The Last Dance

Chapter One

Ivy

"Ivy, did you see him?" Mira nudged me as she bounced in place—which she always did when she was excited—and stared at the retreating back of our star quarterback, Kellen 'I'm God's Gift to Griffin High' Peterson.

I yanked my trig book out of my locker and juggled its heavy weight in one arm while I shrugged my backpack over my other shoulder. Hopefully, I wouldn't be completely deformed with one shoulder six inches lower than the other by the time I graduated.

"No. Who was it?" I asked in an innocent tone. Mira had been hooked on Kellen since the end of last year when some freshman had spilled his hot lunch tray—spaghetti—all over her. Kellen, who had been standing in line behind her, had very nicely helped her clean it up. Instant obsession—just add tomato sauce. I slammed my locker shut with a jarring clang. Trig was out in a portable and I had to hurry to get there on time.

"It was Q," Mira whispered. "He's wearing his jersey because of the game tonight." She sighed. "Number Twelve."

"Quincy Jones is here?" I asked.

Mira scowled at me. Her straight blond hair, complete with a streak of Griffin Eagle's blue, was cut in long shaggy layers that fell over her eyes making her look like an anime character, one of her many obsessions. The ponytails on each side of her head wiggled like little animals trapped in the undergrowth as she fake-smiled at me.

"Very funny. You know Q is Kellen's code name." She narrowed her eyes, making the heavy eyeliner she used look like two black slashes across her face. "Don't pretend you don't know. Oh, and by the way, you're like the only person under the age of fifty who even knows who Quincy Jones is."

"Oh, that Q," I deadpanned, "the quadriplegic."

"Stop that," she hissed. "That is so politically incorrect. What is wrong with you? Q is for—" she paused, searching for the right adjective— "for the quintessential quarterback," she said with a dramatic fling of her arm. She was wearing blue fingerless gloves and smacked some guy who was behind us right in the face. "Oops, sorry."

I rolled my eyes. "In case you didn't notice, Q the Fabulous is still going out with Laurel Simmons."

"Temporary insanity," Mira said airily. "Mark my words, he won't always want to date a cheerleader."

I glanced pointedly at her combat boots, blue and white striped over-the-knee socks and skimmed up to her blue skirt and white blouse with the blue cami peeking from underneath. I raised my eyebrows. "You think he's going to go for militant English school girl soon?"

"That's *sexy* militant English school girl, thank you very much." She propped her hand on her hip. "And yeah. Why not? He just doesn't know me yet."

Lily Jenkins rushed by as we walked the other way down the hallway. Freckles covered her nose making her look younger than her seventeen years. The fact that she was one of the last seniors to still wear braces didn't help. Her red curls bounced wildly around her head. "See you guys tonight!" she cried. "I'm so excited!"

"Be there at five," Mira called after her.

"C'mon." I linked my arm through hers. "Hurry up—I've got to get all the way out to portable three. I thought you said you had a class with Q."

"I do." She sighed. "French. I'm just not sure if he knows I'm in the same room or not."

"Make that the same planet." I laughed, dodging around a couple holding hands in the hallway.

Mira made a point of perusing my teal-colored North Face jacket. I was wearing a pair of skinny jeans tucked into grey suede boots that laced up the back. My outfit was the same basic uniform of probably one hundred other girls in school, which was fine by me. Mira's lip curled in disgust. "At least I'm different."

I shook my head. "You're wasting your time, Mira."

She pointed her nose in the air. "Ivy, stop being so practical. Someone's got to believe in the power of true love. Isn't there anyone out there who makes your heart zing when you see them?"

I shook my head. Mira was the romantic, not me. Who had time to look for true love with the academic load I was carrying? My parents had a dream for me: to be a doctor. I didn't dare disappoint them—even though I had a different dream to study music. But I did wonder sometimes if I would ever fall in love. My older brother was a senior in college, also working to be a doctor, and he still hadn't had a serious girlfriend. We were a practical family. Did people like us find true love?

I adjusted the strap of my backpack to a more comfortable position. "Sometimes practicality is under-rated. Which is better—lusting after an impossible dream or settling for reality?"

"Never settle." Mira waved her arms and spoke in a lofty voice. "Dreams are the stuff that our lives are made on…"

I curled my nose. Drama was Mira's favorite subject and she was always quoting passages from well-known plays—usually incorrectly. "Dude, was that supposed to be Shakespeare? Because that was totally messed up."

"Hush." Mira snapped her fingers at me. "That was loosely paraphrased from The Tempest and you know what I mean."

"*Really* loosely," I laughed. "Why don't you stalk somebody like Tank Bergstrom who at least knows you're alive?"

Mira snorted. "In case you haven't noticed, Tank is in love with his electric guitar. I don't want to break them up." She flipped her hair as she turned the corner, the blond ponytails flying.

I smiled as I turned the other direction. "See you after school."

AFTER THE FINAL bell rang Mira and I met at the locker to grab our homework before heading to the back parking lot.

"Yes!" Mira cried, thrusting her hands into the air as we escaped into the late September sunlight. The sky was a brilliant blue with one long white vapor trail cutting across it—fading proof of someone's escape from the mundane life in Small Town, USA. She skipped across the asphalt, her arms flung wide. "Freedom!"

The mood seemed to be contagious. Everyone was celebrating the fact that it was Friday and the Homecoming game and dance were tonight. Kids were yelling and joking. Music was blasting from a black Nissan. A couple of guys were throwing a football across the parking lot.

"Ivy, look out!" Mira squealed.

I looked up just in time to see the pointy end of the football coming straight at my face. This was not going to be pretty. Before I could react, a large hand reached in front of my nose and snatched the ball out of the air.

The owner of the hand stepped in front of me just in time to see my mouth drop open in a horror-stricken expression. With an effortless swivel, he turned and flicked his wrist, sending the ball sailing back across the parking lot in a perfect spiral without spilling a drop of the open can of cherry coke he held in his other hand.

"Sorry about that," Q the Fabulous said as he looked over his shoulder at me. The mischievous grin that quirked the corner of his gorgeous mouth, however, negated his apology. It was obvious he'd enjoyed scaring the shit out of a complete stranger. He jogged away without a second glance.

"Oh my God, he saved your life," Mira breathed in my ear. "Isn't he fabulous?"

"Saved? I was almost maimed for life," I muttered, still wondering what he found so humorous about that near-death experience. "And he looked like he enjoyed it."

"But still—he was close enough to touch."

I rolled my eyes. "Please Mira. Don't make me barf."

We threw our backpacks into the back seat of Mira's vintage orange Volkswagen Beetle. It was some European model her father had driven back in the day, with silver sections over the tires. The wheels even had matching orange rims. We climbed in, slamming the doors shut behind us.

"Come on, Jefferson," Mira said to the car as she turned the key and pumped the accelerator. Mira's license plate started with JCB so we'd named the bug Jefferson Christopher Beetle. "Fire that engine up, baby." The car rumbled to a start. Mira ground the clutch and we jerked our way into the line of cars to exit. Mira was a bit stick-shift challenged, even though Jefferson was the only car she'd ever driven.

Neither of us lived far from the school and it was only a few minutes later that she was dropping me off at my house. "Be a good girl and get all your chores done so your Mom's not p.o.'d, okay?" she called as I climbed out of the car.

"Yeah, yeah."

"I'll pick you up at four-thirty to go to the game."

"IVY! HAVE YOU practiced yet?"

I ignored the yelling from downstairs and flipped the page of the People magazine.

"Ivy." I jumped as my mom suddenly appeared in the doorway to my room. I hadn't heard her come up the stairs. She could be sneaky like that. "I asked you if you'd practiced yet?" Her dark, shoulder-length hair was just beginning to show streaks of gray.

"I practiced this morning, Ma. Before breakfast." I flipped another page and eyed the spread of gowns for some award show, wishing she would go away. But I knew better.

"You practiced your violin this morning. I'm asking about the piano." Her voice was firm, with just a hint of an

6

accent. Nineteen years in America was not long enough to erase the threads of Vietnamese that clung to her English. "You've got an orchestra concert in a few weeks and Mr. Flynn wants you to play the showcase piano piece. You need to practice so you don't embarrass yourself. Plus, it will look good on your application when you apply to medical school." She moved down the hall. "And it wouldn't hurt to practice your violin again too. Is your math done?"

My mother's voice faded and I slapped the magazine down on my legs. What my mother really meant was 'don't embarrass your parents.' Practice piano, practice violin, AP classes, homework, excel, excel, excel. My parents were unrelenting in their efforts to give me a better life and more opportunities than they'd had. My uncle was a well-known surgeon in New York and they'd decided in pursuit of *their* American dream that both my brother and I would follow in his footsteps. What I wished I could tell them was that in the process, however, they would probably kill me.

I stared at the poster of The Eiffel Tower that hung on the wall across from my bed. Mira and I had cut out a picture of Jefferson and taped it to the poster. Paris. Some days I wanted to ride a vapor trail there. Away from the pressure to be me—future Dr. Ly.

I returned to my magazine and eyed a picture of Nicole Kidman and her husband, Keith Urban, posing at some gala. Sleek and beautiful. My gaze shifted over to the shimmery pale lavender gown that hung from my closet door. My dress for the dance tonight. It would have been fun if I'd been asked to my last Homecoming dance, but I hadn't so I was going with Mira and two other girlfriends. In four years of high school I still hadn't had a real boyfriend. Not that I had time for one. Not that I'd met anyone who I wanted to be my boyfriend. Not that my mother would let me have a boyfriend. But *still*.

And Brandon Chang didn't count. Maybe he *was* super cute and had a 4.0 GPA to match mine, but I'd known him since fourth grade. He was like the male version of me. I swear he'd been in every orchestra, advanced placement math and science class I'd ever taken. We even got our braces off on the same day.

It didn't matter that he used to like me. He got the same pressure at home to excel that I did. Nothing good could come of a relationship where both parties were neurotic over-achievers. Besides, he was going out with Jenny McNamara now. And I was counting the minutes until I could escape to college.

Mira hadn't had a real boyfriend either. But that didn't stop her from crushing over them constantly. Though she'd been hung up on Kellen Peterson for a record-breaking amount of time, I wasn't convinced Q the Fabulous even knew she was alive.

"Ivy!"

With a groan, I slid off my bed and headed down the stairs. The truth was, I didn't mind the music practice. It was all the nagging that went with it that bothered me. The invitation to play the showcase piece for our symphony concert was quite an honor. It made me nervous and excited at the same time to think of performing the complicated music for others to hear.

As I sat down at the piano my father poked his head into the room. "Be a good daughter and do as your mother asks, Ivy." He softened his words with a smile. "Besides, I always enjoy listening to you play."

"I know, Pop." I smiled at him as I ran my fingers over the keys, enjoying the ripple of notes that flowed like a river of music. I loved the piano. That was my dream. To make music my career. I'd said something like that to my mom once. Her response? 'Ivy, music is entertaining but medicine is a higher calling. You study music now to better comprehend medical school later.' It didn't do any good to talk to my father because he always went along with my mother. I'd never brought it up again.

I lost track of time as I played, concentrating on an intricate passage until my fingers knew the notes better than my brain. The music soared through the room and filled me. It was more than an hour later when I stopped.

"Was that an hour?" My mother called from the other end of the house where she was cooking chicken curry with coconut milk. The aroma made my mouth water.

"I have to get ready to go, Ma," I yelled back. "Mira's picking me up at four-thirty. It's the game and dance tonight, remember?" I took the stairs two at a time, trying to escape before she brandished a spoon at me to make me practice longer.

I pulled on a maroon scooped-neck t-shirt over my white lace cami and ran a brush through my long dark hair. I scrubbed my teeth and checked for anything green that might be stuck between them. It still surprised me how perfect and straight they were, even though I'd had my braces off for almost two years. The same old Ivy stared back at me: Large brown eyes, a tiny nose, surprisingly high cheekbones, a good jaw. It would have to do. Some things practice couldn't improve.

My journal was sitting on my headboard. Had I left it out? I grabbed the bound pages and looked at what I'd written this morning: *Homecoming tonight.* I stared at the words for the longest time, a weird jumble of emotions running through

me. Nine more months and I'd be done with high school forever. No more Homecomings. No more classes with Mira.
A pang pierced my chest. What did my future hold? Was it
my parent's plan for me—to be a pre-med student at an Ivy
League college—or was it something different?

I ran my finger over the words I'd written. It seemed like
my journal entry needed something more—sort of like my
life—but I couldn't think of anything to add so I slammed
the book shut and hid it under my mattress.

I lifted the skirt of my gown as I walked by and let it float
back into place. The embellishments glittered in the light
and something inside me felt glittery and excited.

I wondered if Brandon would be at the dance.

Chapter Two

Kellen

"Kellen!"

Charlie Jackson, my favorite wide receiver, jogged toward me in the hallway. He was wearing the same blue and white football jersey that I was, in a show of team spirit for the game tonight. He raised a tattooed arm and knuckle-bumped my fist as he fell in alongside me.

"You got your mojo workin' for tonight, bro?" His eyes were level with mine, one of the few guys in high school tall enough to claim that perspective, as he slapped me on the back. "We're countin' on you to work your magic for the big dance."

I grinned at him. The whole team called our games 'dances'—it was a tradition borne from baseball and the big show. "CJ, we haven't lost a Homecoming dance in eight years. It isn't gonna happen tonight either." I flexed my chest

11

and arms. "The Griffin Eagles gonna soar, baby." There was a beautiful vision of glory on replay in my mind. I was hoping there'd be some college scouts in the stands tonight. Since I'd started playing youth football at eight years old my dream had been to play quarterback in the Pac-12. I was so close to making that dream reality.

"Now, that's what I'm talkin' about. I'll catch you later, man." Charlie flashed his pearly whites at me, almost as bright as the diamond studs in each of his ears, before he jogged off in an easy lope. Kids smiled as I walked down the hallway.

"Good luck tonight, Kellen."

"Show 'em how to play ball."

"Take no prisoners, dude."

I nodded at the well-wishers, slapping a few hands in high-fives, enjoying the attention. I was the quarterback of the football team. I dated Laurel Simmons. Life was good.

"We'll be cheering for you, Kellen." Emma Jacobson gave me a flirtatious smile, shaking her hips in her little cheerleading skirt as she walked by. I grinned as I looked over my shoulder to catch the backside of that action. Emma had 'matured' in the last few years, if you know what I mean. That's when I saw Laurel at the other end of the hall. Her long blonde hair was tied up in a ponytail with a blue ribbon to match her cheerleading outfit. We'd been dating for a year and even though things had been rocky between us the last six months, I had big plans for the homecoming dance after the game.

She had her back to me as she pulled a book out of her locker. I sneaked up and grabbed her around the waist, pulling her off balance against me.

"Hey baby," I whispered in her ear.

She let out a shriek of surprise before she whipped around to face me. Never shy, her lips locked on mine with a vengeance. Part of me wondered if her response was for Hailey and Caroline, who stood watching. Laurel liked to be the center of attention now. But I didn't care.

"Ahem." Somebody cleared their throat behind me.

"Excuse me, Mr. Peterson, but I believe you should be in third period right now." I straightened up at the sound of Mr. Decker's voice. "Please release Miss Simmons and proceed to class."

Short and thin, with a receding hairline and glasses, our principal was actually a pretty cool dude. He definitely went easy on the football team so I didn't want to rock the boat. I let go of Laurel and looked over my shoulder to smile down at the older man.

"I was just leaving, sir."

His lips stretched in an indulging smile. "Good plan." He made a shooing motion at Laurel. "You too, Miss Simmons. I'm sure you two will see each other later." The principal continued past me. "Good luck tonight, Mr. Peterson. Make Griffin proud."

"I plan to, Mr. Decker," I said, as I sauntered down the hall. I was livin' the dream.

Little did I know, that night was going to be my last dance.

THE AIR IN the locker room was electric, like a mini-thunderstorm brewing in that small, sweat-filled room. There was always a lot of excitement before a game but the one against Bellevue was the biggest of the year. Twenty years ago, due to over-crowding, the school district had split Griffin High School into two schools. Half of the students had gone to Bellevue High, a new school on the other side of town. With that one move, the district had created an insane cross-town rivalry. It was almost like they'd split the family in half. But it made for good football.

The pent-up tension was enough to power the lights in the stadium as the team got their game face on. Coach Branson was tough, a grizzled ex-pro defensive back, and he worked his players hard. He was old-school, but he was fair. Part of the Never-Say-Die club. He wasn't a man of a lot of words but what he said meant something and he had our respect.

"How many of you want to win tonight?" Coach looked around the room. The short parts of his salt and pepper hair that stuck out from beneath his Griffin Eagles hat were mostly salt now.

A roar went up in the locker room.

He pointed a crooked finger at each of us, one at a time. "Do you want to win, Oliver?"

Ollie clenched his fist in front of his chest and gave it a pump. "Yes sir, coach!"

"And you, Kellen?"

Coach had pulled me aside after fourth period to let me know that he expected several college scouts in the stands tonight and made it clear they were there to see me. One step closer to the dream.

I knuckle-bumped Ollie. "Absolutely, coach."

He went around the entire room. "If each of you gives it your all tonight—we'll win." Coach Branson shook his head. His nose looked as if it had been smashed against his face more than once. "We won't score with every play. We won't stop them every time." He tapped two fingers on the table. "But if each of you tries your best, *every* time—we'll be winners. Whether our score is higher than theirs or not."

He held out both his stubby hands toward us. "Because the difference, gentlemen, between winning and *being* a winner is in never giving up. Try again, give it your best every time—and I guarantee—you'll all be winners."

I LIFTED MY right arm like I was throwing a pass as I adjusted my shoulder pads. I was ready to blow the socks off any scouts who might be watching. This was my night to shine—I could feel it.

"Kellen." My best friend, Ollie Walker, came up. He was naked, walking around with that strut of his like he was the cock in the hen house. He bumped shoulders with me. "Tonight's your night, bro. Keep your eye on the target, man, and we'll protect you." At 6'2" and two hundred and sixty pounds, Ollie was the biggest offensive lineman that Griffin High ever had. "We got your back, baby."

I grinned at him. I was taller than Ollie but about seventy pounds lighter. And the seventy pounds he had on me? All muscle. If he ever wanted to take me down my only hope was if I could outrun him. I shook his hand and bumped his shoulder back. "I'm countin' on you, bro." I raised my eyebrows at him. "Is Jazzy going to Laurel's before the dance?"

Something flickered across his face. "Nah, her mom let Jazzy off work to watch the game, but she has to go back in for an hour and help close up the beauty shop. We'll meet you at the dance." Ollie moved on to bump shoulders with CJ and I reached into my locker for my socks.

I knew Ollie's girlfriend, Jasmine, didn't really like Laurel. She'd even tried to get me to break up with her a few times with the old 'you're-too-good-for-her' routine. I gave a mental shrug. Laurel wasn't everybody's cup of tea. She'd been sweet and shy when we'd first started dating, but since she'd become a cheerleader she'd changed. She was really into the whole social thing now. But damn, she was fine to look at and better yet, she liked to make out.

OUR BREATH CAME OUT in smoky clouds as we jogged toward the field. The game had an early start—five o'clock—so we could have the dance right afterward. The gym was booked for some other event on Saturday so those budget-minded wizards at the school admin office had decided to have the Homecoming game and the dance on the same night.

I glanced up at the bright lights of the stadium as I waited to bust through the large piece of paper where the cheer-leaders had painted an eagle flying with a bobcat in its tal-ons. The scoreboard read Home with a big zero under it and Visitor with another big zero. I wondered what the board would read at the end of the game. I imagined an outrageous final score: Home – 42, Visitors – 14 and my lips stretched in a confident grin.

I swear the ground shook from the stomping in the stands when we ran onto the field. We broke into our warm-up for-mation and I threw some passes to CJ. My arm was loose, my legs felt strong—I was ready.

The air was cool, the lights were bright and the band was loud and proud. Right then, they stopped so the crowd could shout '*tequila!*'. It was a picture-perfect night for football. I couldn't wait.

THE GAME STARTED and we quickly scored twice to Bellevue's one touchdown in the first half. Our nickel defense was holding tough against the Bellevue quarterback's strong passing arm and we held them going into halftime.

Bellevue came out with new intensity in the second half and quickly tied the game up. We were halfway through the fourth quarter when Coach made the decision to use the West Coast offense, which was a series of short passes to any of the five eligible receivers. You had to move fast and think quickly when playing the West Coast. My throwing arm was one of my strengths, so this would give me a chance to show off a bit in front of any college scouts who might be watching.

We broke huddle and I dropped back, my fingers tight on the leather of the ball. I scanned the field. Dillon was in motion and CJ had double coverage. I could see a guy coming toward me out of the corner of my right eye. Decision time. I pumped once toward CJ then let it rip to Dillon. The defender coming on my right was blocked by one of our offensive line. Dillon cut hard right and pulled the ball out of the air. A roar went up in the crowd and a familiar surge of adrenaline shot through me. We were driving the ball down field and the goal line was in our sights. We could do this.

"Kellen, we got your back, baby," Ollie said to me when we were all in the huddle. The positive energy was palpable. My offensive line loved it when they had a shot at receiving a pass. I rattled off the play. We broke and hustled to the line.

I called the snap and dropped back to hand-off to one of our running backs. He gained a few yards up the middle. My next pass was incomplete when a Bellevue defender interfered with CJ. We happily took the fifteen yard penalty. That put us on the thirty-five yard line and first down. Time to pull back into the lead.

We broke huddle and I called the snap. I was in the zone—everything was moving in slow motion. I fell back out of the pocket, my fingers tight on the pebbly leather of the football. I stutter-stepped, looking for a receiver. My offensive linemen were in motion and I spotted several easy targets.

I pumped the ball, my arm coiled with power. Out of the corner of my eye I saw that CJ, with his blinding speed, had moved past the fifteen yard line down on the far side of the field. He broke hard left and was open. I turned toward him and rifled a perfect spiral.

I watched to see whether I would hit CJ in the numbers, totally focused. Then the world exploded. A defender hit me square in the back. His helmet was like a sledgehammer as he slammed into my ribs. My head snapped back as I was propelled forward.

The ground screamed up at me like some freaky fast-forward movie. My helmet slammed into the turf. For a fleeting second I smelled the grass and tasted dirt.

Then everything went black.

Chapter Three

Ivy

It was a crisp fall night and the stadium was already packed when we got there. The huge lights that lined the field made it brighter than high noon and the band was playing a rousing song about tequila. It seemed everyone in the stands knew that one lyric and felt compelled to shout it at the top of their voices. Whatever.

In the good news department, Lily and Shelby had saved us seats in the middle of the senior section, although 'seats' was a misnomer because nobody actually ever sat during a football game. All that wild enthusiasm over watching people ram their heads together like modern-day Neanderthals was apparently too exciting to take sitting down.

In the four years I'd gone to Griffin High, this was actually only the second football game I'd attended, the first being more of a learning experience when I was a freshman. I quickly learned that once was enough with football for me.

Mira got me here tonight only because we were all going to the dance later—and basically she begged.

I WINCED DURING every play for the first half when the player's helmets collided with a jarring *crunch,* the sound echoing across the field. Didn't that hurt?

At the end of the first quarter, I convinced Lily and Shelby to go walk around a little bit, just to break up the monotony and see who was there, but Mira wouldn't budge—she wanted to watch Kellen Peterson in action.

WHEN WE RETURNED twenty minutes later, Mira was still glued to the game. She was wearing a blue and white Griffin Eagles letterman's jacket that looked like it was forty years old, but was actually kind of cute—in a vintage sort of way. She held two sad little stick pom-poms in her hands that she'd wave every time Kellen did something. Even if he fell down. It was pathetic, really. I decided an intervention was called for.

As I nudged Mira I noticed that Tank Bergstrom was standing on the other side of her. Interesting. He seemed to be around a lot lately. I wondered if Mira had noticed.

"See that cheerleader down there?" I pointed to the row of six very attractive girls who stood in front of our section waving blue and white pom-poms. They were wearing identical tight white sweaters that looked like they'd shrunk in the wash, with a blue eagle centered across their chests. Super-short skirts that didn't cover any part of their legs completed the ensemble on this 45 degree night. It made perfect sense. "The blond in the middle with the long legs?"

"You mean the one who's so proud of her eagle?"

I nodded at Mira. "That's Laurel Simmons. In real life? *Still* Q's girlfriend."

Mira scowled at me. "Things happen, Ivy. People change. *Anything* is possible."

"If you're delusional," I muttered.

In response, Mira waved her pom-poms and yelled "Go Eagles!" She kept a play-by-play monologue going in my ear, talking into one of her pom-poms like it was a microphone even though I didn't understand half of the football terms she used.

"And Peterson drops back from the huddle, looking—no receivers in sight. He's running right under pressure, he pitches a lateral to the tight end Tuiasosopo," her voice rose with excitement, *" and Tuiasosopo breaks over the line of scrimmage and he's down. Five yard gain on the play. And it's second and five."*

On the next play she continued. *"Peterson drops deep—looks—pumps once, throws the ball to Jackson and—"*

Q was tackled from behind and smashed to the ground, face-first. Mira gasped and gripped my arm until I could feel her fingernails through my jacket. "Oh, shizzle!"

Chapter Four

Kellen

I think I might have been unconscious for a few seconds, but there were three guys piled on my back so I had a few moments to get it together. Steve Largent Lesson Number One: Never show weakness.

When the last guy got peeled away from me I pushed off the grass and hopped to my feet. Luckily, Ollie grabbed my elbow and held tight when I wobbled.

"You okay, man?" Our helmets were bar to bar and I could see the worry in his eyes. "You got your bell rung good, baby."

"Yeah, I'm okay." I shook my head and immediately regretted it as white hot pain lanced behind my eyes.

"Shit, we should've been protectin' you, man," Ollie said. "God damn Josh let that guy through. I'm gonna kick his ass after the game."

"Just go kick some Bobcat ass and that'll be enough," I said. I blinked my eyes a few times to try and clear my head before I leaned into the huddle to call the next play. A defender had knocked the pass away from CJ's hands so we were still on the thirty-five yard line with four minutes left. Should be easy to score.

Bellevue saw it differently however, and they blocked our passing as well as our field goal attempt. Coach came up to me as I jogged off the field.

"You okay there, Kellen?" His watery blue eyes were surrounded by wrinkles and topped by two bushy grey eyebrows that always reminded me of fuzzy caterpillars.

"Yeah, I'm fine." My head hurt and I kept blinking to clear my vision, but I was okay. Besides, whining didn't get you anywhere in football.

"Good job out there." Coach slapped me on the back. "We're going to have time for one or two more drives when we get the ball back and here's what I want you to do." He lifted his clipboard and started sketching out a play. I nodded as my gaze followed the lines and circles that his red pen drew. I knew every play in our playbook by heart—I should've known just what he wanted me to do, but for some reason the route lines look unfamiliar.

Our defense held the Bobcats at bay and I snapped my chin strap into place as I jogged back onto the field. It was now or never. I bent over into the huddle and looked at all the eyes staring at me intently. For a second they all looked like strangers. I tried to recall the play that coach wanted us to execute but my mind was blank.

"Didn't coach say he wanted a stop route on the first play?" CJ asked.

"Yeah." I pretended that I'd been just about to say that. "CJ and Dillon go down and hook. Get as far as you can— I'm gonna let this one fly. Break."

The guys fanned on the line of scrimmage. I called the snap and backed up. My offensive line did a good job of buying me time. I watched CJ out of the corner of my eye but his defender was tight on him. I pump faked his direction then let loose with a bomb down to Dillon.

My throw was right on the money and Dillon caught it going away. It truly was a thing of beauty. The pass floated over his left shoulder into this arms and he ran into the end zone. The crowd erupted into a frenzy of celebration. I thrust my arms into the air in jubilation as my teammates ran toward me.

The final score was Home—21, Visitor—14. Not exactly what I'd visualized but good enough for me.

THE LOCKER ROOM was a mad house with guys whooping and yelling. They peeled their jerseys off and threw them into the air. Music blasted from somebody's ihome and Coach was soaked from the ice bucket that had been dumped on his head.

He was still dripping when he motioned at me. Instead of waiting, he turned and headed to his office, high-fiving the guys as he went.

I was only wearing my pants when I stuck my head around the corner of his open door.

"You wanted to see me, Coach?"

"Yeah Kellen, come on in for a minute." He waved me in. "And shut the door so we can hear ourselves think."

I clicked the door shut and slid into one of the hard black plastic chairs in front of his desk.

"What's up?"

He pushed his ball cap back, revealing a tan line from his hat across his forehead, his expression serious. Something turned in the pit of my stomach. Then his face split into a wide grin. "I've got three Pac-12 scouts who want to talk to you, Kellen. The University of Washington, Washington State University and Arizona State University. " He thumped the desk with his closed fist. "You played a great game tonight, and they all saw your talent." His eyes gleamed with excitement. "You can write your own ticket from here, son. Just be smart."

Coach stood up and held out his hand. I jumped to my feet, his words just starting to sink in. College ball. I was going to play college football. It was a dream come true. It was *my* dream come true.

"I'm proud of you, young man. You're an example to every player on this team about hard work and dedication." He wrapped his big meaty paw around mine and shook. "Keep it under your hat for now. They'll be contacting you over the weekend, I'm sure. I just wanted to give you a heads up."

"Thank you so much Coach." I repeated myself several times. It was the only thing I could get out of my mouth.

"I'll call your parents later and talk to them. Go over the game plan of what to ask these guys. But for now—get out of my office." He grinned at me. "I think you've got another kind of dance to attend."

"Yes sir. Thanks, Coach." I hustled out of his office in a daze. I was going to play college ball.

Chapter Five

Ivy

After the game, Shelby, Lily and I got dressed at Mira's house, fondly known as the Mansion. Her father owned a software company that provided products to Microsoft. That's why she lived in a big Tudor style house in Springwood, one of the nicest neighborhoods in town.

"Ivy, will you curl the back of my hair?" Shelby held the curling iron out to me. She was already dressed, wearing a gown the color of pink bubble gum with a halter strap neck-line and BIG cascading skirts of pink tulle. Tall and thin, Shelby was painfully shy. Between her blond hair and pink gown I wondered if she knew she looked like Barbie come to life.

"Sure." I shoved my last bite of Hawaiian pizza into my mouth. I wasn't the most adept at using the curling device as my hair was about as straight as hair can get, but I rolled and released Shelby's hair until ringlets hung all over her head in a pretty mess.

"Do you think I should stuff my bra?" Mira asked as she stood in front of a full-length mirror on the back of her closet door and shoved a sock down the front of her baby blue strapless dress. Her hair matched her dress. One side of her bodice stuck out in a lumpy sort of way making her look lopsided. "I'm so freakin' flat you can't even tell I'm a girl," she complained.

"That's not true." I said. "You're svelte, in a glamorous sort of way."

Mira propped her hands on her thin hips and stared at me in the mirror. "What's glamorous about being flat?"

"Keira Knightly's flat," Lily said, from where she stood in front of the adjoining bathroom mirror applying her tenth layer of mascara. She was still wearing her yoga pants and a ripped Griffin Eagles t-shirt, her red curls pulled back in a ponytail. Her dress of pale green silk hung on a hanger from the door behind her. Though she had been in dance programs since she was a toddler she still battled her weight and frequently complained about being a late bloomer. "She's glamorous."

"She's British. That's all you need." Mira stuffed a sock in the other side of her dress. "Don't you think I look better with a shape?"

"What if one of your socks falls out while you're dancing?" I couldn't help myself. My mother had drilled practicality into my head from a very young age. I took a bit out of a new piece of pizza. "That could be sort of... um. mortifying."

Lily giggled. "But memorable."

"Yeah, what if some cute guy asks you to dance and your sock slips and suddenly your boob is coming out of your stomach?" Shelby snorted with laughter. "I think you should wear them just to see what happens."

Mira yanked the socks out of the front of her dress. Her dress sagged slightly over her small chest. "You're right. Better not risk it." She raised her eyebrows at me and I knew what she meant was that she didn't want to risk looking stupid in front of Q. I wanted to remind her that Q was going with a date and wouldn't even know she was there, boob-in-the-stomach or not, but why burst her bubble?

I finished putting on makeup, which was minimal—a little eyeliner, a little mascara— and pulled on my dress.

"Oohhhh, Ivy." Shelby had caught my reflection in the mirror where she was now painting her lips bubble-gum pink. Her blond ringlets swung as she turned. She stared at me with glowing eyes. "That gown is perfection on you." She strode over and lifted the shimmering lavender overskirt making the sequins and beads glitter in the light. An underskirt of deep purple made the top layer seem that much more ethereal and magical. The gown was strapless with a beautiful wrap that matched the overskirt. "It's so fancy—" she hesitated. "I'd never guess you'd pick a gown like that. You're usually so—"

"Practical?" I said.

"She didn't pick it." Mira called in a muffled voice from inside her closet where she was pulling on her boots. She poked her head out the door. "I picked it. It's her Cinderella gown and she's going to meet her true love at the dance tonight."

Even though it was a joke, there was a tiny part of me—one I barely let myself acknowledge—that wished it were true.

Chapter Six

Kellen

The mood was more than festive at the Homecoming Dance—it was exhilarated. Nothing like a last second win to pump up a crowd who didn't need pumping up in the first place. Ollie and CJ had scored some Jose Cuervo so we had a few shots to loosen us up before we entered the gym where the dance was being held. Laurel looked fantastic in a short black strapless dress that barely held in her curves, which was fine by me.

Even I had to admit that Laurel had changed in the last twelve months. She used to be kind of shy and sweet, but after she made the cheerleading squad in her junior year and we started dating—she definitely gained some confidence. The clothes she wore now emphasized her figure and showed off body parts that just seemed to get bigger and better, if you know what I mean.

I surveyed the crowd. The theme of the dance was A Night in Paris and the gym was decorated with what looked like a million sparkling stars glittering from the ceiling. The decorating committee had hired CJ's dad to build this really tall, 3D lighted Eiffel Tower which looked amazingly real from a distance. Especially after a few shots of Cuervo.

"Let's get our pictures taken by the Eiffel Tower now, Kellen." Laurel tugged at my arm. "You know, in case we want to leave early," she added with a seductive whisper. That was all it took to get me on board. The photographer had this fake black moustache glued to his lip and an outfit that I guess was supposed to be from the turn of the century, like he was some French artisté. But it did the trick, because he looked so cheesy it was easy to smile.

The flash of the photographer's camera was still bright in my eyes, obscuring my vision, when Laurel chirped in my ear, "Want to dance?" We had a real band, a group of seniors who'd been playing together for a few years, and the dance floor was packed. I kept blinking away the light residue but it took a full minute for my eyes to clear.

"Nice game, Kell!" Brian Matson called over, giving me a fist pump. His girlfriend gave me a warm smile. Really warm.

"Your arm was on fire tonight—way to stomp the Bobcats, bro." Johnny Tuiasosopo, our big Samoan tight end, waggled his little finger and thumb as he gave me the hang-ten hand sign. His long black hair was pulled back in a ponytail and hung longer than most of the girls here tonight, but his family was like football royalty in Washington, in both college and pro ball, and included several well-known players. There was never any question about his athletic talent.

"Thanks, man." I jerked my chin at him and instantly regretted it as pain lanced through my brain. I wished the Cuervo would stop the kick-ass headache that was trying to split my head open. So far it only seemed to be making it worse.

"Kellen." Emma slid up close to me, winking at Laurel, before she rubbed against my arm. She was wearing a short red dress that showed off her legs and from my perspective, a lot of cleavage. "You're my new hero. Awesome game tonight."

'Yeah, thanks, Em." I pressed the heel of my hand into my right eye and rubbed my forehead. Damn, I did not feel good.

"Go find your own boyfriend, Emma." Laurel laughed as she pulled Emma away from me. They'd been cheerleaders together the last two years and were good friends.

Rid of Emma, Laurel danced with enthusiasm in front of me. I shifted my weight from one foot to the other but the music reverberated through the gym, rattling my head. I scanned the doors trying to decide which one I could sneak out if I needed to take a break from the noise. I was so tired it was all I could do not to just lay down right there on the floor.

The band kicked into one of my favorite John Mayer songs. Even though the song had a fast beat, Laurel slid into my arms and pressed against me, burying her face against my neck.

"You want to slow dance, don't you?" she whispered.

I closed my eyes and tried to enjoy the moment but my head was pounding so hard it felt like somebody was running a drill hammer on my skull.

I stumbled and Laurel caught me. She gave me a suspicious look. "Have you been drinking?"

"Who me?" I gave her a lazy half-smile, faking my innocence, because she knew damn well I had. But not enough to be staggering.

She stepped back and put her hands on her hips. "Why wasn't I included?"

"Social piss, remember? All the girls had to go at the same time." I shrugged, holding my hands out from my sides. "That's when the booze showed up."

Laurel had the grace to smile at that, because she knew it was true. Sometimes the girls would be in the bathroom together for thirty freakin' minutes. Doing what, no guy knew. Nor did we want to know.

"What've you got?" she pressed. "Beer?"

"Tequila," I replied. "To kill ya. And it's not mine. It's CJ's."

Laurel had her hair up in an elaborate hairdo that was cemented into place with hairspray. I was starting to feel sick to my stomach and for a second I wished her hair was down so I could close my eyes and bury my face in the softness.

"Do you think he'll share?"

I shrugged, wondering why the tequila was bothering me so much. We'd gone to dinner before we came to the dance. I had plenty of food in my stomach and hadn't had that much to drink. "Probably."

"Let's go then." She smiled up at me, her eyes full of promises. "I'm ready to party."

Fresh air and less noise sounded good to me. At the moment, however, the look in her eye was more than I could handle.

"CJ's over there with Ollie." Laurel pointed across the room. "They're talking to Ivy League and her lesbian friends."

I could see CJ in his black tux all slicked up for the dance. He had his hair in corn rows and his earrings sparkled in the light. Dressed like that you couldn't see the tattoos that lined his arms with a few sprinkled on his chest and back for good measure. He was surrounded by four or five girls who looked tiny next to his tall frame. Pink, blue, and green dresses— they blurred together and looked like sugary pieces of candy. I shook my head to clear my vision. One girl had even dyed her hair to match her dress. That took some nerve.

A blond girl in a very large pink dress moved and I spotted the girl who Laurel had been talking about. Her gown was darker, almost iridescent, and fell in simple lines to the floor. With her tan skin and cloud of dark hair she looked exotic and mysterious. With a start, I realized I knew her. She was in my AP English class.

"Why do you always call her Ivy League?" I asked. "Her last name is Ly."

"Because she's a geek, that's why." Laurel motioned with her hand as though she was shooing a bug away. "And of the eighteen hundred kids in this school, Ivy Ly will probably be the only one who'll get into an Ivy League school." Laurel's nose curled. "It's just what she is."

"What do you mean?" For some reason my brain was in slow motion tonight. "She's in my—"

Laurel sighed and rolled her eyes before she cut me off. "I mean she's just so Ivy League. She's a bookworm, music major, and a math geek all rolled into one. Haven't you ever noticed? She's a walking stereotype." Laurel tugged at my hand, pulling me through the crowd toward CJ. "And she came to the dance with three girls. Explain that."

"Maybe she doesn't have a boyfriend and wanted to enjoy the last Homecoming dance of high school." I let

Laurel drag me across the floor. "I really don't think that's any big deal." Frankly, I didn't care about the geek girl. I just wanted my headache to stop. The stars overhead were glittering in a freakin' weird way. I squinted, trying to focus on them.

I wondered if I was going to throw up when puke suddenly spewed out of my mouth. The next moment the gym floor came rushing up at me in the most impossible way. I heard Laurel shriek, "Kellen!" before my forehead smashed into blackness.

Chapter Seven

Ivy

The dance was crowded when we arrived. The gym had been transformed with glittering lights and a giant Eiffel Tower stood in one corner. Old streetlamps were lined up to form walking paths and umbrellas were strewn about the floor as if a rain shower had just passed. It was wonderful.

I'd always dreamed of going to Paris and the sight of that glowing Eiffel Tower and the sparkling stars hanging from the sky made me oddly giddy inside—like there was magic in the air.

We'd barely got in the door when I heard a stunned voice say, 'Ivy?'

I turned and there was Brandon, staring at me with his mouth half open as if I'd grown two heads. I did a quick check to make sure I wasn't having a wardrobe malfunction but he managed to recover and croaked, "You look beautiful."

My cheeks started burning and for a second I had a total out-of-body moment like I'd never met the guy before. He wore an elegant white silk tie with his tux instead of the standard bow tie he had to wear to the orchestra concerts, and apparently he'd gotten contacts because the black frame glasses he usually wore were gone tonight.

"Oh, hi Brandon." I made a point of looking around so I didn't stare at him with the same shocked look he had on his face. I'd never seen him look so good. "Where's Jenny?"

He jerked his head away as if he'd just realized he was devouring me with his eyes and pointed toward one of the other doors. "Bathroom."

"Oh." I pointed across the gym. "The Eiffel Tower looks good, doesn't?"

'Yeah, Charlie Jackson's dad made it. Supposed to be an accurate scaled down version." He shoved his hands in his pockets and shuffled his feet. "They've got a photographer that's supposed to look like—"

Mira grabbed my arm. "Hey, Brandon. C'mon Ivy." The next thing I knew we were headed across the gym. The band started playing another song and the sounds of their electric guitars filled the gym.

I heard Brandon shout, "See you later, Ivy," but all I could do was wave over my shoulder.

"I want to get my picture taken by the Eiffel Tower," I yelled at Mira. "I'm going there in real life one day."

"Well, duh. Me too." She was fixated on something across the room. "We'll do it later though."

The band was loud and a few couples were dancing but most were standing in small groups talking. Or rather, yelling.

"Where are we going?" I shouted over the music to Mira.

"Shelby and Lily are talking to Jazzy." She pointed to the other side of the dance floor. "I had to come back for you. Let's catch up with them." Part of me wondered if Mira had sent them to Jazzy, knowing her boyfriend, Ollie, was Q's best friend, and figured Q would eventually meet up with them. But it didn't matter, I was just there to have fun with my friends. If Mira wanted to pine over Q that was her choice.

WE'D ONLY BEEN talking to Jazzy and Ollie for a few minutes when Mira grabbed my arm, her fingers pinching my skin. I could feel her bouncing as she stared at something behind me like a dog on point. It didn't take two guesses to figure out what.

"Oh my God, he's right there," she whispered.

I turned to look and Q puked all over the front of my gown.

IT WASN'T A surprise that some of the football players had been drinking. Q must have been one of them. He puked on me then passed out on the floor. They had to call the medics and take him away in an ambulance. Mira was a wreck. In fact, Q's girlfriend, Laurel, held it together better than Mira did. To be honest, she seemed more pissed that her party had been cut short than worried about Q.

After they took him away, Mira, Shelby, Lily and I went into the bathroom to do damage control but it turns out you can wash puke out of a skirt, but not the smell. I didn't have any choice but to leave. After watching Q collapse, Mira didn't want to stay either. Shelby called her dad and he said he'd come and get her and Lily later so, with their blessing, Mira and I headed for the parking lot.

When we got to Jefferson, Mira climbed in and reached across the seat to unlock my side.

"Roll down the windows," she said as she started the engine. "You stink, girlfriend."

I was somewhere between laughing, crying and gagging over the smell as I manually rolled down the window. Gotta love those vintage cars.

"This is not how I imagined this night going," Mira said in a small voice.

I looked down at my water-stained skirt that had been so beautiful just an hour before. My lower lip trembled and I bit down hard to force the tears away. "Yeah." My voice sounded rough. "It's funny—I don't remember Cinderella getting puked on in the story."

Mira laughed and pointed to my wrap where I'd left it in the back seat. "At least part of your Cinderella dress is still clean."

I looked back at the beautiful lavender fabric as Mira shifted the car into gear and pulled out of the parking lot. Moonlight glinted off the sparkly parts and a single tear rolled down my cheek. It didn't seem like any part of my life ever went according to my plans.

Chapter Eight

Kellen

It was the annoying beeping that woke me up. Why was my alarm clock going off? I never set that thing. I opened my eyes and looked around, planning to pound the shit out of it. A TV was mounted near the ceiling and a white board was on the wall in front of me with the words "Nancy" written in blue ink. I turned my head and looked out the wall of windows to my right. There was an expansive view of tree tops. Where was I?

"Kellen, honey." My mom ran her fingers over my forehead. There was a tone in her voice I'd never heard before. Relief? Fear? My father stood just behind her, staring at me. "Do you know who I am?"

I scowled at her. What the hell kind of question was that? Black circles colored the space beneath her eyes. My mother always looked like a million bucks, but right now her hair was pulled back in a headband and she wasn't wearing any makeup. The only time I saw her like that was when we were at the lake.

"Off courth," I slurred. I tried to push myself into a sitting position. That's when I realized I had wires and tubes attached to me.

"Don't sit up yet." My mom pushed on my shoulders to keep me down and suddenly I was wide awake. The annoying beeping started going much faster and with a shock I realized it was a heart monitor. For *my* heart. "You've had an accident. You're in the hospital."

"Wha?" I croaked. My mouth felt like I'd just spent an hour in the dentist's chair.

"It was at the football game. You bumped your head and…" her voice dropped off and she pressed her lips together. My father put his hand on her shoulder. His other hand was resting on the white blankets that covered my left leg.

My dad cleared his throat. "There were complications, son."

I DON'T REMEMBER much of anything about the Homecoming Dance. I remember being with Laurel and getting our picture taken in front of that crazy Eiffel Tower with the corny Parisian photographer dude with the fake moustache. I remember Laurel going on about some girl she thought was a geek. But that was it. My mom told me the dance had been a week ago.

Yeah. A WEEK.

Freaky, right?

Apparently, the tackle where I'd gotten sacked—gotten my 'bell rung' as Ollie had put it—had injured my brain and two arteries had started to bleed. They call it a closed head injury. That's why I had such a killer headache at the dance. My brain was bleeding.

They also called it intracranial hematoma.

Try to say that ten times fast.

Turns out, I can't even say it once now. The words are just fine in my head but I can't seem to get them out of my mouth. It's like half of my tongue is numb. Or like I drank a bottle of Cuervo on my own. I figured it must be the painkillers they have me on.

"HI HONEY, how're you doing today?"

I opened my eyes at the sound of my mom's cheery voice, even though the morning sun made my head hurt. Her bright orange sweater didn't hide the black circles that still shadowed the skin under her eyes. I wondered if she ever slept anymore. She stayed in the hospital with me until ten p.m. every night and was back at seven a.m. the next morning.

"Dad had to go into the office this morning but he'll swing by later this afternoon and check on you." She leaned over the bed rail and smoothed my hair back so she could kiss my forehead.

I closed my eyes. I swear my mom had aged ten years since the Homecoming game. And my dad—he acted all upbeat and kept saying '*you can handle this, son*', but there's this look in his eyes—like he'd seen the depths of hell or something. It scared me.

I'D BEEN SLEEPING a lot the last few days. The only visitors they let in were my mom and dad. Occasionally, Dr. Murdoch came by and checked things. She asked me all sorts of ridiculous questions. And she wanted me to move my arms and legs, but that didn't go so good. My right side—my throwing arm—seemed to be affected the most.

"Can you move the fingers of your right hand, Kellen?"

I stared at my hand as I tried, but my fingers only twitched. It was like a circuit had been disconnected between my body and my brain. Like my arm belonged to somebody else now.

"Um hum," Dr. Murdoch said, like not being able to move your freakin' hand was no big deal. "What about your right leg?"

At first, I'd tried to convince myself that nothing serious was going on, just a bad concussion or something. But I didn't believe it anymore. I gritted my teeth and lifted my head off the pillow as I grabbed the silver bed railing. It was all I could do to shift my leg on the mattress. Dr. Murdoch scribbled some notes on the chart. A terrible fear that had been slowly gnawing at my insides suddenly bubbled in my stomach until I thought I was going to be sick. I couldn't deny it anymore. This was bad. *Really* bad.

"TIME TO GET out of bed, Kellen." The nurse bustled into my room and began unhooking the assortment of beeping machines that were attached to me. I checked the white board. Her name was Suzy. In purple ink. Suzy draped the cords over the machine and released the safety bar from the side of my bed. "Roll up to a sitting position and swing your legs to the side of the bed."

My right arm was no support as I pushed into a sitting position. I could swing my left leg just fine, but my right leg only partially got the message and dragged across the sheets. I wanted to slide my hand under my knee and lift my leg up, but my hand was too weak.

"Let me help you with that, dear." With surprising efficiency, the nurse stretched over the end of the bed and lifted my right heel. "Just swing around this way." Then she gently lowered my right foot to hang next to my left. "Hold on to the bed when you stand and just take your time. I've got you on this side." I pushed myself out of bed and stood up. Suzy slid close to my right side and put her arm around my waist. Her head just reached my shoulder.

I wobbled and reached for the handrail on the bed, but Suzy had released it to the floor so I could get out of bed. I could barely keep my balance. It was like my right leg was made of jello. My arm wasn't much better. Thank God the nurse was holding me up or I would have done a face-plant faster than you could've said '*what a dumbshit.*'

I STARED AT the silver walker that stood next to my bed. It was the same freakin' thing my grandma used to use. Even down to the sliced green tennis balls on the front legs. They wanted me to 'walk' the floor of the hospital with a walker. Supposedly it was just until I built up my strength and coordination again, but I wasn't so sure. Because I'd tried it—twice now—and it was all I could do to get around the entire floor and back to my room. WTF has happened to me?

I WAS STARVING when lunch came. It was spaghetti, which sounded really good. I forgot about my gimpy right hand and reached for the apple juice. The cup slipped out of my fingers and spilled all over the tray and onto my blankets. What a freakin' mess.

After the nurse, Kathy in green ink, got that cleaned up I tried to eat but I couldn't manage. As soon as I lifted the fork, the pasta slid off. I finally got so frustrated that I cleared my entire lunch tray with one swipe of my arm. The tray, the plate, the tin dome lid and the food all clattered to the floor in an explosion of sound. Spaghetti sauce went everywhere. Talk about making some noise.

Embarrassed and guilty at the same time, I mumbled 'sorry' which came out sounding like 'sawy' before I turned on my side. I stared out the window while Kathy and some other nurse cleaned up *another* mess of mine. I never used to have a temper but now I'm so angry all the time.

THEY LET COACH in to see me today. He took his ball cap off as he approached my bed, like he was at a funeral or something.

"How you doin', son?" He looked so sad.

"Goo Coash." I closed my eyes at my garbled speech. Shit. Coach's usual gruffness couldn't hide his pity. For a second I thought I was going to cry.

"Don't worry, Kellen." He patted my shoulder with that big hand of his. "Don't you worry about a thing. You concentrate on getting better." I couldn't decide if his encouragement made me feel better or worse.

I wanted to ask Coach about the scouts. I wanted to ask him if I would start when I got back to school. I knew Mark Carter must be starting quarterback now.

But I didn't.

I just nodded and said 'yeah.'

THEY LET OLLIE and CJ in to see me.

"Hey, buddy. How ya doin'?" Ollie sauntered in with that easy walk of his and leaned over the bed guardrail to grab my left hand to shake it. I wondered if they'd told him about my right hand because he'd never grabbed my left hand before in his life.

"You're lookin' good, Kell, won't be long before they kick you outta this joint," CJ said as he stepped up next to Ollie. His hair was picked in a 'fro today which made him look even taller than he already was. They both looked so good—so strong and healthy.

I just nodded and gave them a thumbs up. I hated to admit it, but I didn't want to try and talk in front of them and sound like an idiot because my speech was still messed up. So I just nodded and said 'yeah' occasionally, and hoped that maybe they wouldn't notice.

"Coach is letting Carter start, but just as a filler until you get back," CJ said. "We really needed you last week against Northside. Hansen's field goal kicks were the only thing that saved our asses."

Ollie leaned his elbows on the bed's side bar, the muscles flexing in his arms. "And Jazzy said to tell you hi." He mock-punched me in the shoulder. "She wanted me to give you a hug and a kiss, but I'm gonna pass on that one."

I pressed my lips together and tried to hold back my smile, because my lips didn't move like they're supposed to anymore. Something flickered in Ollie's eyes and then he blinked to hide it. I think he could tell.

It was only a few minutes later when he pushed off the railing and nudged CJ.

"Well, we better hit the road, bro. They told us not to stay in here too long and interrupt your beauty sleep." A wave of relief washed over me. I was exhausted just trying to hide how fucked up I was. "We wanted to check in and let you know we're here for you, buddy." He put his hand on my leg and patted my left knee, his skin dark against the

45

white of the hospital sheets. His voice got soft. "Hang in there, man."

"Yeah, let us know if you need anything, Kell," CJ added. "I mean, *anything*." His voice wavered and he sort of looked like *he* was trying not to cry.

"Thanks." The word came out garbled, but I'm pretty sure they understood me.

Ollie raised his hand as they walked out the door, then flipped it to a thumbs up. "We'll see you soon."

I returned the thumbs up with my left hand. Once they were out the door I turned to stare out the windows at my elevated view of a nearby forest. My hospital room was high enough that I could see over the tops of the trees, like a bird in flight. But the reality was I couldn't even walk on my own two feet. I blinked against the sudden pressure in my eyes. Ollie and CJ's visit reminded me of the one thing I'd tried not to think about: I hadn't heard from Laurel.

Chapter Nine

Ivy

Mira rushed up to me in the school hallway, her eyes wide with excitement. There was a hot pink streak through the blonde hair that swept across her forehead that matched the hot pink dotted mini and black fishnet leggings she was wearing—complete with hot pink boots. I was in skinny leg jeans, black boots and a black shirt. Somebody had to balance her flamboyance.

"Ivy—" she clutched at my arm, her hands encased in hot-pink fingerless gloves— "did you hear that Kellen Peterson got out of the hospital?"

I kept walking. There was barely enough time to navigate the crowded halls of Griffin High and get to my fourth period orchestra class within the four minutes they allotted us. I definitely didn't have time to stop and chat.

"The quarterback?" I didn't dare make fun of him now. My crack about Q the quadriplegic still rang in my ears with an uncomfortable resonance, because from everything I'd heard, the dude was seriously messed up.

"Of course." Mira hurried along with me. "How many Kellen Petersons do you think go to this school?"

Before Kellen's accident I hadn't really given the star quarterback much thought other than to listen to Mira prattle on about him. But now, it was pretty gut-wrenching what had happened to the guy.

We were both seniors. He was in my AP English class. Eight months and seventeen days and we were all out of here. I was bound for college—if my parent's got their wish it would be either Stanford, Harvard or Yale. That is, if I survived playing Mozart's Piano Concerto No. 5 in D Major next weekend as the showcase piece of our Fall symphony concert. I wondered what the future held for him now.

"Q was in a coma for a week after the game."

Mira knew I was not a fan of football. In my opinion, it was a stupid game where the main goal seemed to be to try and hurt the other player. I knew about Q's condition because that was all Mira and anybody else had talked about for days after the game.

Mira adjusted the black sparkly messenger bag slung across her shoulder she used as a backpack. "They wouldn't let anybody see him. They had to drill a hole in his head to let off the pressure. I heard they think he had a mini-stroke."

I flicked my long bangs to one side so I could get a better look at her face. "The way you keep track of him and talk about him all the time, you'd think you were his girlfriend." I nudged her with my elbow, trying to get her to look at me. "Don't you think you should leave it to his real girlfriend?"

Mira averted her eyes. "His real girlfriend is a bitch."

I frowned. Mira didn't swear very often. She made up imaginary swear words instead, like 'shizzle' or 'holy chicken head'. I cleared my throat. "Apparently he doesn't think so."

"That's because he doesn't know." She glanced over her shoulder to see who was behind us in the hall before she continued in a whisper. "I heard that Laurel's been seeing Josh Hendershot behind Q's back." Mira made a hissing noise in the back of her throat. The sound always reminded me of a vampire but it was her way of verbalizing her utmost disgust. "Cheating on someone while they're in a coma—that is seriously cold."

"Yeah. Downright bitchy." I, on the other hand, had no problem with swear words. I looped my arm through hers and pulled her around the corner into the commons that led to the orchestra room. "But the good news is—it's not our problem."

Chapter Ten

Kellen

I had to go home in a wheelchair. It was like my brain wasn't connected to my body anymore. The docs scheduled me for physical therapy five days a week because I need to strengthen my right arm and leg. Not to mention my fingers. My handwriting looked worse than a first grader's.

They also gave me a journal. A going-away present, I guess. Told me to start with today and write something every day. But I started with the day of the homecoming game. That's when everything changed.

Usually I only write a line or two because it takes forever, though it's hardly legible. My right hand won't work and I can't write for crap with my left. I guess this way I don't have to worry about anyone reading it.

Thank God I could communicate with my friends by texting. Sort of.

I kept hoping this was all a nightmare and maybe I'd wake up.

MY MOM TOOK another week off work to stay home with me and drive me to physical therapy since I couldn't drive my truck yet. The work-outs were grueling, but I was used to it after all the years I'd trained for football, basketball and baseball. At least I could take my frustration out on the machines. But in the end, they always kicked my butt.

Then there was my homework. Ollie and CJ were taking turns bringing my assignments over to the house for me. They knew how bad things were now. How my leg and arm were messed up. How tough it was to talk clearly. They promised they wouldn't tell.

I'd discouraged anybody else from stopping by, though it was nice to know so many people cared and wanted to help. Some of the kids from school even put up a 'Welcome Home Kellen' banner across our front porch.

School had always come easy for me. I had a decent grade point average—a 3.8— because I wanted to have options after football. Secretly, I'd always toyed with the idea of being a doctor one day. After my football career, that is. But I'd never killed myself to get straight A's, though I'm pretty sure I could if I wanted. Now, I can't seem to remember anything I'd read and trying to think my way through a simple math problem gave me a headache.

At this rate, I'd be lucky if I kept a 2.8 gpa.

LAUREL CAME BY TODAY.

I had just returned from PT so I was really tired. When I got tired, nothing seemed to work very well. My right leg dragged, my fingers wouldn't do what I wanted and my speech was more slurred than usual.

I was flopped across the couch, watching ESPN, still in my sweats and pitted-out t-shirt. I was too tired to try and navigate a shower.

My mom answered the doorbell. I could tell when she came into the family room and cleared her throat that it wasn't CJ or Ollie. I pushed myself up with my good arm and peered over the back of the couch.

I'd never seen Laurel look better than she did right then. Her blonde hair was brushed back away from her face as if blown by the wind. We'd had a stretch of sunny fall weather and she was wearing a pair of beige shorts and a light blue jacket. Her legs were long and tan. As she walked toward me it was like one of those slo-mo moments with the babe on the sports commercial.

"Hey." I tried to push myself into a sitting position without looking clumsy. I was acutely aware of how perfect she was and how far from perfect I was.

"I just couldn't wait one day more before I saw you," she cried. Behind her I saw my mom roll her eyes before she left the room. Laurel slid onto the couch and faced me, reaching for my hands. "How are you?"

"Good." I nodded. I kept my right hand close to my body so she couldn't see how weak it was. My fingers curved into my palm now and my wrist was twisted in a weird way. I wondered what she really saw when she looked at me. I'd lost quite a bit of weight and I knew that my cheekbones were more pronounced than they'd been before. I had a problem with the right side of my mouth— when I smiled, my lips didn't always match up. So I tried not to smile.

She waited for me to say something but when I didn't she looked down and fidgeted with the zipper on her coat. "When are you coming back to school?"

I concentrated on making my words clear. "Maybe in a week or two." I nodded again. I could do that much normally. I think. My fingers ached to touch her skin, to wrap my arms around her and bury my face in her hair. Just to be normal again. Do all the things I used to take for granted.

But I didn't move.

"How've you been?" I managed to ask.

She got a weird look on her face that I couldn't figure out. "Fine." An awkward silence filled the space between us making the distance seem unbridgeable.

She asked a few more questions. Was I in pain? Had I been doing my homework? Did I know Mark Carter was starting quarterback now?

I gave short awkward answers. My heart pounded and ached at the same time. I wanted to ask her what she'd been doing. How cheerleading was going. Anything. Everything. Mostly I wanted to ask why she hadn't visited me in the hospital. But I didn't.

She looked at me for a second, then dropped her eyes.

Another long silence stretched between us.

"Well, I guess I better go." She jumped to her feet.

I nodded. "Yeah." I couldn't stand up without giving away how bad my right side was. I was tired enough I wasn't sure my right leg would support me. "Thanks for coming by." But even to my own ears my words sounded garbled and confusing.

Her eyebrows flicked into a brief frown and then she forced a smile onto her face. "Well—" she lifted her hands up and let them drop to her sides— "take care. I'll see you soon." She backed away from the couch. I lifted my left hand to wave goodbye as she turned and walked out of the room. I stared at her legs as she left, long and tanned—working so effortlessly.

When the front door snapped shut behind her I closed my eyes and let my head drop back against the couch. A long sigh slipped past my lips and I squeezed my eyes shut to try to stop the tears from escaping.

What had happened to my life?

Laurel sent me a text an hour later breaking up with me.

Chapter Eleven

Ivy

My mother adjusted my hair and straightened the collar of my white shirt. Again. I was an odd mix of nerves and calm. I knew this piano piece inside and out. I had practiced until my fingers were raw nubs of flesh. Okay, that was an exaggeration, but it sounded good.

As I stood in the antechamber off the main auditorium I listened to the swell of music as the violins, cellos, and flutes crashed into a crescendo. Eight more measures and they would stop and introduce me. I flexed, then wiggled my fingers to keep them limber. I wondered if anyone had ever had a heart attack and fallen face first onto the keys whilst playing Mozart's Piano Concerto No. 5 in D Major?

"Remember to smile," my mother instructed me. "All your hard work will pay off."

The music came to a halt and applause echoed through the room. I began to pace, a wave of nerves trying to drown me. I heard the voice of the conductor over the microphone.

The door creaked open and a woman dressed in black stuck her head into the room. She motioned with her hand. "Ivy, you're up now."

I nodded and gave my mother a quick peck on the cheek. My father was seated out in the audience along with Mira, Shelby and Lily, though the girls weren't sitting with my parents. They had come to support me, but at that second I wished the concert hall was empty.

"Make us proud," my mother whispered to me.

I nodded and walked through the door.

"And remember to smile."

A swell of applause started when the audience spotted me. I smiled and nodded in acknowledgement, my shoulders back, as I walked at an even pace to the grand piano centered in the middle of the orchestra. I wondered if I was going to throw up on my dress just like Q did.

The conductor in his black tails bowed to me and spoke soft words of encouragement as I stepped toward the piano bench. I took my seat and faced the familiar row of black and white keys. A calm settled in my shoulders and arms. It was like coming home. I poised my fingers over the keys and nodded my readiness to the conductor.

My fingers knew their way through the song as much from muscle memory as from conscious placement. The melody rippled from the keys and soared to the highest peaks of the room. I forgot the audience. I forgot my friends. I forgot my parents and their dream for me to be a doctor. It was just me, my piano and the musicians around me, speaking a language that flowed through my fingers rather than through my mouth.

Thirty minutes later I finished with a flourish and was greeted with deafening applause. I knew my mother would have heard the few mistakes I made, but apparently the audience hadn't, because they gave me a standing ovation as I left the room.

Brandon Chang was first cello and caught my eye as I walked by. He raised his eyebrows and gave an approving nod. It was like ten pounds had been lifted off my shoulders. Playing piano, creating music—this was what I wanted to do with my life.

Chapter Twelve

Kellen

"Welcome back, Mr. Peterson." Our principal, Mr. Decker, sounded sincere as he walked around his desk to greet me. It had been a month since I'd been to school. I could walk on my own again, but my right foot dragged in a weird way if I tried to walk fast. Well, really, if I walked at all.

Mr. Decker started to reach for my hand to shake then thought better of it and put his hand on my shoulder instead. "Per your parent's request I've taken the liberty of lining up a tutor so you won't have any trouble getting caught up on your studies."

I nodded.

"If you need any help with anything—" he paused to look me in the eyes— "and I mean *anything*, son—you let me know."

"Thank you, sir." I ducked my head as I spoke so he wouldn't see my lips twist in that weird way they did now. I used to think I owned this school. Now I wanted to be invisible.

He motioned to a chair in front of his desk. "Have a seat. She should be along any minute."

She? My tutor was a girl? Shit. Great.

The principal slid a hand over the few wisps of hair that covered the bald top of his head. "I've arranged for her to accompany you to your classes for the next few weeks so she can take notes and get you back up to speed."

He picked up a piece of paper and glanced at it as he sat down on the edge of his desk. "It looks like you've already got a class together—AP English—maybe you know her?" He looked up at me. "Ivy Ly?"

The name sounded familiar but I had trouble remembering my own name lately, let alone matching faces and names with people I barely knew from classes I hadn't attended in a month.

I shrugged and shook my head.

"Ah, well, that may be all for the best. Miss Ly is a brilliant student. She's maintained a 4.0 all four years she's been in high school while taking accelerated classes. She's also a gifted musician excelling in both violin and piano." He peered closer at the paper again. "Hmmmm…it looks like she's going to be working with you fifth period on the piano as well."

Mr. Decker glanced up at me. "Do you play?"

I shook my head, trying to ignore the headache that was working its way up from the base of my skull. Though I had taken four years of piano lessons when I was younger, I hadn't played since I was fourteen. I wasn't even remotely interested in playing music now, unless it was the tequila song they played at the football games.

But Dr. Murdoch had insisted there was new research that suggested playing the piano not only helped the brain generate new synapses to replace those damaged by the injury, but also helped with finger and hand dexterity. That was all it took for my parents to sign me up. It didn't matter what I thought.

There was a hesitant knock before the door to Mr. Decker's office pushed open. A face peeked around the corner, her long dark hair swinging off her shoulder.

"Mr. Decker? You wanted to see me?"

"Yes, Miss Ly—" the principal motioned with his hand for her to enter the room— "thank you for coming so promptly." He retreated from his perch on the side of the desk and sat in his big wooden chair. "As I mentioned in my email to you, I've had a request for a tutor and I think you fit all the requirements quite admirably. Let me introduce you to Kellen Peterson."

I lifted my left hand in her direction, not even trying to smile. Instead, I wondered what she saw when she looked at me. I used to be Kellen Peterson, star quarterback of the Griffin Eagles. Had she known who I was? And even if she did—who was I now?

Mr. Decker swung his hand back toward the girl— "and Miss Ivy Ly."

I'd definitely seen her before. She was small-boned and pretty. Really pretty. She had dark—almost black—hair and tan skin. Her eyes were equally dark and alive with intelligence. I could almost feel it crackling as she swept me over in one flick of a glance. She couldn't hide her surprise either. It was obvious she hadn't known what she'd signed on for.

Mr. Decker glanced down at the page again. "Miss Ly has completed a number of the classes you're in—math, science and fourth year French—so she can assist you in getting back up to speed on the content you've missed. Additionally, she'll accompany you to your other classes for the next few weeks. Luckily, you both have sixth period study hall."

Luckily. I looked at my new tutor again. She was very petite and wore skinny leg jeans that just emphasized how small she was. She stood ramrod straight with her hands folded in front of her like she was lined up for inspection. Her face was expressionless as she stared at Mr. Decker and I wondered what she was really thinking.

Mr. Decker looked up from the paper. "Ivy has also generously agreed to stay after school if you need extra assistance on homework, if necessary." He smiled at both of us. "Sound okay?"

I just nodded. It was too much to try and tell them I wouldn't need her—I had physical therapy after school every day. They probably wouldn't be able to understand me anyway.

I glanced at Ivy out of the corners of my eyes again. She didn't look any happier about the situation then I did. Basically, she was there to wipe my butt because I was too messed up to do it myself. I got the feeling she'd summed me up and filed me away before I'd even had a chance to open my mouth and slur my words.

God—what did I do to deserve this?

Chapter Thirteen

Ivy

God, what did I do to deserve this? When Mr. Decker emailed me and said he wanted to talk to me about a community service project that would look good on my college applications I'd been pleased he'd picked me. Honored, really. He'd mentioned it involved tutoring but teach a stroke victim? Or whatever Q was? Are you kidding?

I was shocked by how thin he was. Kellen Peterson had always been big. Big shoulders, muscular arms, tall, athletic and good-looking—and he knew it. He'd always strutted down the hall like he owned the school. The kid I was looking at now was too thin, his cheekbones pronounced, his clothes hanging on him. There was something defeated in his eyes.

The Q that Mira had babbled on about had kept his hair shorter, like all the jocks, but this guy's hair was long and shaggy, like Tank Bergstrom's. It swept across his forehead and shadowed his eyes—almost like he was hiding behind it.

Don't get me wrong—he was still good-looking—but in a very different way from how I remembered our star quarterback.

"So, now that you both have your new assignments—" Mr. Decker got up and opened the door— "might as well get to it." He gave us a big smile. "Let me know if you need anything."

Q barely acknowledged me when we left Decker's office. He mumbled something I couldn't quite understand.

"What?" I leaned forward to hear better, but I couldn't understand him the second time either. I didn't dare ask him to repeat it a third time but I thought he said, 'Sorry to get you involved."

My sympathy didn't last long. When we got to our first class, everybody—and I mean *everybody*—in that room seemed to know him and wanted to welcome him back. He slouched into a chair and tried to wave people off but it was like the serfs paying homage to the returning king. Sickening, really.

I just stood there like I was invisible.

And he just ignored me.

Brilliant.

AT LUNCH TIME he went to sit with all his jock friends. I was so relieved to be rid of him I practically ran to find Mira. Once we were through the lunch line I pulled her outside to tell her the news. I didn't want to take the chance that we would be overheard by anyone.

I set my brown lunch tray on the outdoor table and plopped down on the cold wooden seat, pulling my black pea coat tighter across my chest. "Don't freak, okay?"

"Why are we out here?" Mira looked at me like I'd lost it. She was in electric blue skinny pants with knee-high black boots today and a black and white striped t-shirt underneath a black jacket. She looked like some freakish rock star. In a fashionable sort of way.

"It's like 40 degrees," she said. "And in case you haven't heard, Kellen Peterson is back at school. I want to go stare at him while we have the chance." She glanced toward the windows of the cafeteria as she spoke. "Have you seen him? He's so thin."

"I need to tell you something." I gave her my piercing 'this is important' stare that any true friend would instantly recognize. Mira, however, ignored me.

"Do you think he's been sick too? Maybe that's why he's so thin."

"Listen." I growled.

She frowned and her eyebrows became slashes across her forehead. "What?"

I tugged at her arm. "Sit down. I don't want you to faint when I tell you."

Her butt hit the wooden bench like it'd been pulled down by a giant magnet. "I don't like the sound of that. Tell me what?"

I held up my hands to placate her. "Don't panic. This actually might be your golden opportunity."

"Now, you're starting to make me nervous. Just spit it out—whatever *it* is."

I cleared my throat and spread out a napkin. I'd known Mira since first grade. We were closer than sisters because we never fought. Potentially until now, that is.

"Decker called me into his office this morning." I picked up my bagel and concentrated on spreading some cream cheese on one side.

"Oh." Her voice got lighter. "Are you getting an award for your grades?" Mira didn't have the same pressure at

64

home to get good grades. Nor was she driven enough to seek them on her own. She always said she liked to live vicariously through me.

"No. I'm not getting an award." I thought about what I did get and it seemed more like a punishment than anything. "I have to tutor somebody—go to their classes for five periods then work with them during study hall. And maybe after school occasionally," I added in a rush.

"Whoa." Mira jerked her head back in surprise. "What's Decker going to do—give you a time-turner?" Mira was a complete Potterhead. She quoted Harry Potter like it was the gospel.

I snorted and dropped my bagel back on to the plastic wrap. I'd lost my appetite just thinking about it. "He said something about the teachers agreeing to make an exception and letting me do my homework on an extended schedule. It should only be for a few weeks," I added hurriedly. I had a feeling that would be a crucial bit of information for her to know.

Mira's face twisted into a mask of confusion. "Who needs a tutor for that much of the day? Are they a foreign exchange student or something?" All of a sudden she put two and two together. Her mouth sagged open. "Wait a minute."

She grabbed my wrist and gave me the 'this is important' stare—which I, of course, immediately picked up on. See—I wasn't such a bad friend. Was I?

"You're not."

I gave a little mouse-squeak of a nod. Then I talked as fast as I could. "I have to tutor Kellen Peterson until he gets caught up in his classes." It was ridiculous that I felt guilty. I tried to shove the emotion away like I'd shoved my bagel away, but the mess was still there in front of me – in both instances.

Mira spoke in a shocked whisper, a smile of delight twisting the edges of her mouth. "You're going to tutor Q?"

"Decker said it would look good on my college applications. Like a community service project or something."

"You're going to tutor Q five periods a day?" She dropped my wrist and her smile faded.

I nodded. "I guess I've taken all of the classes he needs help with but this will be a great way for you to get to know him, too. I was thinking, since you have sixth period study hall too—you could join us. Didn't you say you had a class together?"

"Yes, French." Her eyes narrowed and her lips pressed together.

My stomach clenched at her changed expression. I didn't want her to be mad at me. She was my best friend. It wasn't my fault.

"Mira, it wasn't like I asked to be stuck with the guy," I said. "It's going to be a nightmare. He doesn't want me there anymore than I want to be there. I'm not sure why—"

"Stop." Mira pressed her fingers against my lips and raised her chin. "Don't tell me anymore. It's happened for a reason." She gave me a Holy Mary look. "We're meant to save him, Ivy."

Chapter Fourteen

Kellen

"Kellen?" Mom called up the stairs. "Kellen? Are you up there? It's time to go to therapy, honey."

I was on my back, stretched across my bed. I had a pounding headache and I was so tired I didn't think I could move. I didn't want to move. I heard her footsteps coming up the stairs and I ran the back of my hand across my eyes to make sure they were dry.

I sat up as she entered my room. "I don't think I can do it today, mom."

The look of sympathy that crossed her face was almost more than I could stand. She sat down on the bed next to me and put her arm around my shoulders. "I thought you said school went okay." She was silent for a minute. "Harder than you expected?"

"No." I couldn't stop the anger that crept into my voice. "It was *exactly* what I expected. A freakin' nightmare."

I shoved away from the bed and stood up. I had gotten to where I could balance on my good leg now since my right foot still dragged. "I used to be the quarterback. Now I'm the cripple. You think *everybody* doesn't stare?" I wanted to slam my fist into the wall.

"Kellen." Her voice sounded as pained as I felt. "It was your first day back. You know it will take some time. You'll get back to normal. Dr. Murdoch is very optimistic. It's only been a few weeks since you got out of the hospital. Just allow yourself the time to heal. Everyone will understand."

"And in the meantime—" I knew my words were garbled. When I got emotional I was even harder to understand— "I'm going to lose everything I've worked for my whole life."

"You're not going to lose it, Kellen." Her voice was soft and understanding.

"Yes, I am," I snarled. "I won't be able to play football the rest of the season. I can't see any way that I'll be able to play basketball either." My voice broke. "I may never play any sport again the rest of my life."

My mom stood up and walked over to me. At 6'3 I was almost a foot taller than her, yet I'd never really noticed the height difference before. She was always just mom. She was always the boss—the one who knew what to do to get things done. For the first time in my life it occurred to me that there were some things she couldn't fix.

She rubbed my back. 'If you make up your mind to play a sport—you will. If you make up your mind, Kellen— " she put her hand on my cheek and forced me to look at her— "anything is possible. You just might have to go about it a little differently than you originally planned." Her tone changed. "Now, the only way that will happen is to do your

68

physical therapy." She patted my back. "Come on. We don't want to be late for your appointment."

IN THE END she was right. Even though I was exhausted, it felt good to work out my frustration on the exercise bike. Michael, the therapist, knew how hard to push me and when to back off. He seemed to understand my mood today and let me ride the bike longer than usual. I was grateful that he wasn't quite as tough on the stretching exercises afterwards, though I was sure I would pay another day.

It was dark as we drove home.

"Did you meet your tutor?" Mom asked.

I looked out the window into the black night and against my will imagined Ivy Ly. We hadn't talked much as she followed me around from class to class. She couldn't make it to sixth period study hall today because of some 'previous commitment' so we were going to start tomorrow. Whatever. I didn't have a clue what was going on in any of my classes, anyway. I'm sure she felt as uncomfortable as I did.

During the day my football buddies and a lot of my friends had come up to welcome me back. After they hugged me or high-fived or whatever, they would glance from me to her, trying to figure out why she was standing there. For some reason, I didn't introduce her to anybody. I just ignored her. I knew she felt uncomfortable, but I guess that's how I wanted her to feel.

I let out a long sigh and let my head fall back against the headrest. When had I become such an asshole?

"Yeah, I met her."

My mom glanced over at me. "Was she nice?"

"She was fine." I tried to ignore the sliver of guilt that speared me in the stomach. I had ignored Ivy because she made me mad.

Because she was confirmation of my weakness.

Chapter Fifteen

Ivy

I was exhausted when I got home. Who knew how tiring it was to be humiliated all day?

I pulled my math book from my backpack and slammed it onto the kitchen table. Somehow the loud noise made me feel better. I would never have given into my frustration if my mom had been home, but she didn't get off work as an administrative assistant for the state until five.

I had a ton of my own homework to get caught up on for the classes I'd missed while I'd walked around being Q's personal secretary. I flipped through the pages of my trig book looking for the assignment and tried not to think of how awkward I'd felt half the day standing next to someone who couldn't even bother to acknowledge my existence. I was probably smarter than every one of his friends, yet somehow I stood there feeling completely stupid while they all acted like I was invisible.

My cell buzzed and a text came in. It was Mira.

So? How was it hanging with Q all day? Did he mention me?

I laughed as I read the last part. Mira could always do that – somehow make me laugh when it was the last thing I felt like doing.

Humiliating. He thinks I'm his freakin' secretary.

I set the phone on the table and opened my math book. Our texting conversations usually went on for hours after school. I did homework and nibbled on the carrot sticks my mother had left in the frig for me. Mira watched Ellen on TV and ate Twinkies. She studied vicariously through me. I ate vicariously through her. It was a win-win friendship.

Can't he write anymore?

His right side was affected, so his foot and hand are messed up. And his speech, I think. He doesn't talk to me.

I took a bite of my carrot stick then added another line.

But don't worry – he still thinks highly of himself.

Then I pushed send.

Over the next hour I filled Mira in on the nightmare that was my day. I'm not sure she understood the unpleasantness of the situation. I think she thought just standing in Q's glow was enough to make anyone happy. Pass the barf bag, please.

I was just finishing up my math when my phone buzzed with an incoming text. Mira was on to Oprah reruns now. I wondered what advice she was planning to share today. I picked it up and stared at the message in surprise. It was from Brandon Chang.

Do you want to go to the movies on Friday?

MIRA HADN'T HEARD that Brandon and Jenny had broken up either. We spent the next hour analyzing Brandon and his mysterious text, even though I'd known the guy for-ever. I couldn't believe I'd agreed to go out on a date with him and while I tried to pretend to Mira that it was no big deal, I was oddly excited.

Chapter Sixteen

Kellen

It was just as hard to be back at school the next day. Ollie and CJ were my wingmen though, running interference, but nothing felt the same, now that I wasn't playing ball. Now that I was a cripple.

I ignored Ivy when she sat down next to me in Calculus first period. I was slumped down in my chair with my arms crossed over my chest, my bad hand hidden. I would have given anything not to be in that classroom—not to be at school.

"Hi." She smiled over at me and I noticed how perfectly straight her teeth were. Little Miss Perfect here to help Mr. All Fucked Up. I gave her a short nod and looked away to stare at the front of the classroom instead. Out of the corner of my eye I saw the expression on her face change and she scooted around in her chair and stared down at the desk.

Good, I thought, giving in to my anger. Better than staring at me.

The rest of the day went pretty much the same. She didn't try to talk after that and neither did I. In sixth period study hall she went over the assignments for the day and I just listened. She knew it all, anyway.

THE NEXT MORNING Ivy didn't acknowledge me when she sat down in the seat next to mine first period. I watched her out of the corner of my eyes trying to gauge her mood, but she didn't even glance my way. She just took notes and when she wasn't taking notes, she had another page she was working on—drawing what looked like music. Must have been her own homework, I figured.

For second period science we had to break into groups and work with our partners. Luckily, Dick Swenson, an offensive back, and CJ were in class. They joined our group and covered for me. Dick and CJ were joking about an X-rated text that had gone around about one of the cheerleaders, oblivious to how uncomfortable they were making Ivy. She looked around the room as if searching for a reason—any reason—to escape. A guilty twinge twisted my gut. For an instant it was like I was standing outside myself looking back and seeing what Ivy saw. I didn't like it.

I'D NEVER BEEN so glad to see a Friday in my life. But the truth was, I was starting to get back into the routine again and didn't feel as angry. School was school. Nothing was different there. All the kids made a point of acting like nothing had changed, even though everything had changed for me.

I'd tried to be nicer to Ivy, even though I didn't talk much. I was ashamed of myself the way I'd acted, but apparently she either really held a grudge or just wasn't the warm and fuzzy type. Because the only talking she did was to answer any questions I had on the assignment. I swear she made a point not to ever look at me—like I was invisible. Maybe it was better if we weren't friends anyway.

When Ivy sat down in the chair next to mine in science on Friday, I made an extra effort to be nice to her. I didn't smile, of course, messed up lips and all, but I did say 'hi' as soon as she sat down. She didn't smile either. Just mumbled 'hi' as she got her notebook out.

I studied her out of the corner of my eyes as she was taking notes, wondering what went on in her head. She looked just as normal as any other girl in school but she had to have a super-computer for a brain to be able to keep up with her classes and tutor me on top of it all.

The teacher stopped talking and told us to work with our partners. Ivy slid her notebook over so I could read what she'd written about the project and started explaining what we were going to be doing in class. Her handwriting was small and neat. Her voice was lower than I would have expected and kind of husky, like she'd had too much Cuervo. I laughed in my head. As if.

I scooted my little desk over closer to look at the diagram she'd drawn and caught a whiff of her perfume. She smelled like those white flowers in Hawaii—what were they called? Couldn't remember that either. She was still talking about control sampling when it came to me.

"Plumeria." The word popped out of my mouth like there was a hinge between my brain and my lips. Great. I couldn't remember for shit when I wanted, but nonsensical bullshit poured out of my mouth without any effort at all.

"What did you say?" Ivy gave me a WTH? look but I thought I could see the faintest hint of a blush on her cheeks. So I was right. I grinned at her before I caught myself.

"Your perfume." Now she was definitely blushing. I was just going to tell her it was nice when the door at the front of the classroom swung open. Laurel glided in to deliver a note to Mr. Pruitt and I froze, my eyes locked on her. I'd heard she'd asked Josh Hendershot to the upcoming Sadie Hawkins dance. She looked great in a pair of tight jeans and a white Eagles sweatshirt, her blond hair pulled back in a ponytail. My stomach twisted in the way it used to do before a big game.

I'm not sure if it was my devouring stare or if she knew I was in the class, but after she handed the note to the teacher she glanced straight at me. Her gaze shifted to Ivy and her eyes narrowed in a frown, then she turned away as if she hadn't seen me at all.

Somebody let out a wolf whistle from the back of the room. Laurel turned on her cheerleader smile and tossed her ponytail as she strutted back out the door, one hand on her hip. I was still staring at the spot where she'd disappeared into the hallway when Ivy cleared her throat.

Embarrassed, I looked over to find her eyes on me for the first time since we'd met in Principal Decker's office. Her eyes were dark and mysterious, ringed with thick black lashes. The kind you could get lost in, trying to figure out what she was thinking. When she looked at me in Mr. D's office I could see surprise and a wordless evaluation. Now—I saw pity. I wasn't sure which was worse.

FIFTH PERIOD WE went to the music room and I worked on playing the piano. Talk about death by humiliation. I used to be able to hit CJ in the numbers with a football from forty yards. Now, I couldn't get my freakin' fingers to press down on two keys in the proper sequence to save my ass.

After messing up the same three line song for the fifth time, it was all I could do not to slam my hands down on the keys.

"Listen," I said. My head was pounding and I knew the only way to get it to stop was to close my eyes and relax. "It's Friday, and I'm toast. Do you think we could skip the piano today?" It pissed me off that I even needed to ask her to take a break, but she was trying to help me and I was grateful. "I've got a killer headache and this isn't helping."

"Well—" she hesitated. It was obvious she didn't know what to say.

"In fact, I have a better idea. You must be a piano whiz right?" I scooted over on the bench and motioned at the keys. "Why don't you play something for me?"

"No, no, I couldn't." She looked down at her knees. "That's not why we're here."

"Ah, c'mon, Ivy. Playing for a few minutes couldn't hurt. We'll call it tutoring by example. Besides, maybe it will help me relax enough that I can try again." I leaned my head on my hand and gave her my best puppy look. But the truth was, my head hurt so freakin' bad it wasn't hard to look pathetic.

She hesitated. We were alone in one of the side rooms off the main choir chamber. Nobody supervised us—nobody would care if she played for the rest of the hour—and she knew it.

"Please?" I gave her a half-smile. I'd been practicing in the mirror and if I lifted the good side of my mouth I looked pretty much normal. Laurel used to tell me how much she liked the dimple on that side. "Play me your favorite song."

She looked surprised at that request but she grudgingly stood up. It took me a minute to realize she was waiting for me to get off the bench and switch spots with her. I slid over and took her chair, which was next to the wall, while she sat down on the piano bench.

"I'll just play for a few minutes while you rest your head," she said. "Then you need to try again." Again that look of pity. "It gets easier with practice."

I didn't argue with her. My head was pounding and I felt sick to my stomach. This day, this week, couldn't get over fast enough. "Okay – your favorite song," I said, too tired to care if I slurred my words. "Let 'er rip." I leaned my head back against the wall and closed my eyes, not sure what to expect. Suddenly a thought occurred to me and I sat up. "That is—if you have something memorized?"

She smiled then. I think it was the first real smile I'd seen. 'Lovely' was the word that popped into my head, like something someone would say in a black and white movie. 'Corny' was the word I silently reprimanded myself with. But I was right. She was lovely when she smiled.

"Yes, I have songs memorized." She kind of laughed like she'd made a joke, but I had no idea what the punch line was so I just nodded and sat back again. Whatever. As long as I didn't have to do battle with that piano I was happy.

Her hands rippled over the keys making a waterfall of sound. She moved so effortlessly it was as if the piano was an extension of her fingers. It was a small miracle that the wounded beast I had just been beating to death could now sing like a choir of angels. The song she'd chosen had a haunting melody and the notes told a story that didn't need words. After a few minutes, I closed my eyes again and let the music wash over me. I relaxed for the first time since I'd returned to school.

Chapter Seventeen

Ivy

I peeked over at Q again. He had his head back against the wall with his eyes closed. It was the first chance I'd really had to *look* at him. He was so peculiar all the time: prickly and rude, then stuck-up and distant, then when I least expected it, he'd be charming and sweet. I was trying to be understanding, given the trauma he'd been through, but it was exhausting being around him. If Mira knew the true Q she'd probably run for the hills.

His sun-streaked brown hair was swept across his forehead and the ends flipped out in cute little waves. The way his head was tilted I could see his Adam's apple and the defined line of his jaw. He was very handsome. But his cheekbones stuck out like he'd been sick for too long and now that he was relaxed I could see the dark shadows under his eyes and the lines of exhaustion that aged him behind his seventeen years. An unfamiliar twinge went through my chest.

My fingers rippled over the keys and I was surprised at the song that I'd chosen. It *was* my favorite and not one that I had shared with anyone—even Mira. It was a song I had written. But Q would never know the truth. The melody was sad and sweet and hauntingly beautiful in its simplicity. The song filled a place inside me that I didn't like to acknowledge—an empty place where I hid the things that I longed for. Like true love.

I knew this song well and the notes came to my fingers easily. The music filled the small room and my gaze shifted over to Q again as if I had no control over my eyes. Curiosity killed the cat, I warned myself, but his eyes were closed—he'd never know I was looking at him.

He was wearing a sky blue shirt that made him look tan and healthy. Mira was right. He was gorgeous. Sitting there now, he could be one of those too-beautiful-to-be-true half-naked models they featured in clothing ads for teenagers—except he had a shirt on. But I could tell the chest under that shirt could hold its own with any of those models.

His short sleeves revealed arms that were layered with muscles, even when he was relaxed, but not in a bulky, body-builder kind of way. More in a sleek, gazelle-like sort of way. His left hand was resting on his thigh and I was surprised at how beautiful it was, long and slender, with fingers like an artist. He had the hands of pianist. The thought surprised me and annoyed me at the same time. Whatever. Q was a jock and that was the end of *that* story.

Against my will, my gaze moved to his right hand. It was curled in toward his body, bent tightly at the wrist, the fingers tucked into his palm. The position was in stark contrast to his other hand, with fingers splayed comfortably against his leg. It was as if his body had been divided in half.

When he was relaxed like this, his mouth looked normal, but I'd seen how one side twisted in a weird way when he smiled. Not that he smiled much, but today when he'd blurted out 'plumeria' like he was a contestant on a game show or something, I'd seen him smile before he caught himself. One side of his face had this crazy-cute dimple—

"Ivy."

I jumped in surprise, my fingers faltering on the keys. My cheeks instantly began burning. I jerked around to see who had caught me. I mean called me.

"I knew that had to be you playing." Brandon smiled as he approached from behind. "Nobody can play the piano as well as you." There was true appreciation in his voice as he rolled his black upright cello bag before him. The chair that Q was sitting in was tucked behind a pillar and I caught the surprise on Brandon's face when he spied Q sitting there. "Oh, sorry. I thought you were alone."

"Oh no, it's—uh— " I looked over at Q, suddenly unsure of how to explain the situation. "You know Kellen Peterson, right?" I pointed at Q and then back at Brandon. "And Brandon Chang?" Inside I was dying of awkwardness. Brandon and I were going on a date tonight. Our first date. And it looked like I was sitting here playing a serenade for another boy. What must Brandon think?

"Hey." Q sat up and sort of waved his left hand at Brandon.

Brandon looked as uncomfortable as I felt. "Hey."

There was a long silence. Then Q and I started talking at the same time.

"I'm helping—"

"Ivy's my—"

We both stopped and looked at each other. Something flickered in Q's eyes. Almost like he was laughing on the inside. Now I was sure my cheeks were flaming.

"Ivy's my tutor." Q smiled that half-smile, where the dimple winked in his cheek like he was telling a secret joke. "I'm learning how to play the piano."

"Oh." Brandon kind of laughed and looked at me for confirmation, not sure if the star quarterback of our football team was being sarcastic or not. I gave a mouse-squeak nod. "Okay, well—" now Brandon sort of waved at me. 'Awkward, awkward, awkward' reverberated through my brain. "I needed my cello for this weekend so just came in to grab it." He glanced from me to Kellen and back again. "Right, then." He started to back away. "Ivy, I'll see you about—uh—six?"

"Sure," I nodded, just wishing he'd leave. "That'd be great."

"Okay, then. Bye." He jerked his head at Q and left, pushing his cello bag out of the small room.

"Boyfriend, huh?" Q was sitting up in his chair. He had the strangest look on his face, like he'd never seen me before.

I pressed my lips together and jumped up from the piano bench. "No. We're just going to the movies."

"You're skipping the game?"

"What game? Oh." I'd forgotten the football team had a home game tonight. I shrugged and gave him a feeble smile. "Yeah, I guess so." I motioned at the piano keys, feeling like I should apologize for some stupid reason. "Okay, do you want to try?"

Q pushed himself out of the chair to stand towering next to me. "Nope. I'm done for today. Coach wants me to suit up for the game so my physical therapist said I could come in early." He grabbed his backpack with his left hand and slung it over his good shoulder. "Thanks, Ivy. Have a good week-end." Then he limped-walked out the door without looking back.

BRANDON ARRIVED RIGHT at the dot of six to pick me up. I wondered if I'd be nervous about actually going on a 'date' with him but as soon as I saw him I wasn't. It was the same old Brandon I'd grown up with. Just a lot cuter now.

My mom and his mom were good friends. My mom always commented about 'what a nice boy that Brandon is' whenever she saw him. I'd kind of got the feeling that she wanted to do a little match-making with us, but now that we were actually going on a date, she'd warned me just before he came about not losing my focus.

"Okay Ma." I rolled my eyes. "Just going to the movies. I'll try to stay focused though."

"Don't be flippant with me, Ivy. I'm just thinking about your future. It's only a few months before you head off to college. You don't need any distractions right now." Just then the doorbell rang. Thankfully.

"Hello Brandon." My mom was all smiles. "Congratulations on making first chair in the youth symphony...

Blah blah blah. I grabbed Brandon's arm. "C'mon. We're going to be late."

"What?" He frowned at me, clearly confused. "The movie doesn't start until..." He saw the look on my face. "Oh...right...nice to see you, Mrs. Ly." He nodded at her as I tugged him out the door.

He surprised me by opening the door of his blue Honda Accord for me. He jogged around the front of the car and climbed in the driver's seat. "Too much motherly advice?"

"Waaayyy too much."

IT WAS FUN to be with Brandon. We'd known each other for so long, attending school, musical events and science fairs together as kids, that it was easy to hang out. I wasn't sure if he'd be weirded out about me tutoring Kellen Peterson but he didn't even bring it up. Maybe he thought I was sworn to a code of silence or something, like I'd joined the Jocks-Are-Always-Cool club. But I was happy to let the sleeping dog lie and forget about Q for a few hours.

Really.

Chapter Eighteen

Kellen

Carter threw a thirty-two yard touchdown in the fourth quarter to win the game. Instead of embracing his teammates, he showboated instead. He ran to the sidelines and kissed the prettiest cheerleader. Who happened to be Laurel.

"Dude," CJ said in a tone of utter disgust as we both watched the spectacle, "you should thank Josh for taking that skank off your hands." Of course, Laurel, being Laurel, gave it her all. By the time they were done the crowd didn't know if they were cheering for a football score or for the football player to score. "You're lucky to be rid of her." CJ slapped me on the back and made me turn away, but I'd seen enough to make my guts grind.

"Yeah, whatever," I muttered as Coach yelled for Carter to get back to the bench.

CJ AND OLLIE wanted me to hang out with a few of the guys after the game, but I begged off, saying I was too tired. All I wanted to do was get home and hide in my room. It had been painful to be suited up for the game but incapable of playing. Like being in one of those nightmares you couldn't quite wake up from. Maybe if I played *World of Warcraft* for awhile I'd feel better. Except, oh yeah, playing one-handed didn't work so well.

THE ONLY REASON I left the house over the weekend was to go to my physical therapy sessions. If there was any improvement on my right side it was so miniscule it was immeasurable.

"It's not going to happen overnight, Kellen." Michael, my PT, was a very matter-of-fact kind of guy. He wasn't big, but he was strong and definitely in shape. Plus, the dude knew how to inflict pain. That in itself demanded some respect. "It's just been over a month since the accident. But you're young and strong, if you work as hard at this as you do at football, you'll get it all back and more."

I nodded but I didn't believe him. There was no way I'd ever be back to the level I'd been. I was damaged goods.

AS MUCH AS I prayed for time to stop and Monday to never arrive, it rolled around with annoying regularity. Ivy was already seated when I got to Calculus, just seconds before the tardy bell rang.

"Hey." I dropped my backpack on the floor and crammed myself into the standard issue school desk / chair combo that was definitely not made for football players. Or even has-been football players.

"Hi." Ivy actually looked me in the eye and smiled. She had very pretty eyes – all dark and shiny. She must have had more fun at the movies than I did at the football game.

And that was the high point of class because right after that we were handed back our quizzes from Friday. A big red D stared up at me from the top of the page. I'd never gotten a D on anything in my life.

Out of the corner of my eye I saw Ivy look at the page then turn quickly toward the front of the class. I debated about tearing the paper to shreds or wadding it in a ball. I opted for the wadding and made a nice left-handed throw into the waste basket. Then I crossed my arms, pulled up my hoodie and slid down in my chair. My life sucked.

SIXTH PERIOD FINALLY arrived. It was almost the end of the day and I could escape. Ivy and I were sitting at one of the long tables at the far end of study hall. It was our own little corner and people had learned to leave us alone. I always sat with my back to the room so I wouldn't see the curious glances directed at me like pokes in the ribs.

I blinked in surprise when Ivy pulled out my wadded up Calculus assignment and spread out the creases. "Let's take a look at this and figure out where you got messed up. It's probably just a few simple mistakes." Her tone was straight-forward, reminding me of my mom. Surprisingly, I didn't feel embarrassed about her knowing I got a D. Before, I would have been mortified. For some reason I was more embarrassed about throwing the page in the garbage. Go figure.

"Okay, Ivy Ly, Girl Genius, let's take a look." I was teasing her but her eyes jerked up to mine with a look of alarm. Geez, was I that bad to be around?

She gave me a nervous laugh and pulled my heavy Calculus book closer. "Also, a friend of mine is going to study with us today, okay?"

She was concentrating on flipping through the pages to find the assignment, avoiding my eyes. I frowned. "Who?"

"Her name's Mira." Ivy turned a page without looking up. "Don't worry," she said in a rush, "you'll like her."

I didn't really care if I liked her or not, but what I did care about was for somebody else to see how much trouble I was having understanding and remembering my homework. Ivy was bad enough, but now her friend? I was just about to say not a good idea when Ivy lifted her head and waved at somebody.

"There she is now."

I didn't even have a chance to turn around.

"Hi guys," a perky voiced chirped. The new girl stopped at the end of the table, her books clutched to her chest and a big smile on her face. She looked from Ivy to me then back again. I'm pretty sure she was bouncing in place. "Can I sit with you?"

The new girl's light blond hair was pulled to each side of her head in two long ponytails, and pointy bangs hung down over her eyes. She sort of reminded me of a cartoon character, although it was Halloween and a few kids were dressed up at school. Maybe she was, too. A section in the middle of her hair was colored turquoise – the same color as the fingerless gloves she wore. I narrowed my eyes to get a better look. Who wore fingerless gloves?

"Sure, sit down," Ivy said, with more enthusiasm than I'd heard from her before. She scooted over so the new girl could pull a chair up next to her.

"Hi, I'm Mira." Big turquoise eyes that matched her hair—seriously, she must have been wearing colored contacts—peered at me. She held out a fingerless-gloved hand.

Shit. Hadn't she heard I was a cripple now? I couldn't extend my right arm very easily so I debated about ignoring her outstretched hand, then I thought, oh screw it. She was odd but she seemed harmless. I stuck my left hand out to grasp her fingers in an awkward backwards sort of handshake. "Yeah. I'm Kellen."

"I know." She giggled. "I've had a huge crush on you since last year."

Chapter Nineteen

Ivy

W ho would've thought that after only one miserable week I would be worried about re-inflating Q's super-sized ego? But it was obvious the guy was struggling. Seriously struggling. I'd seen the look on his face when Laurel Simmons delivered the note to our classroom that day. 'Lovesick' was the only word I could think of to describe his expression. Even though he put on a brave face and tried to hide it.

When I brought up Mira joining us, I could tell he wasn't happy at the idea of somebody else spending time with him in study hall—but on the other hand, he wasn't happy about *me* spending time with him in study hall, so what difference would one more annoying person make? Besides, maybe Mira's obsessive fandom would help him. Not to mention that maybe she'd stop asking me about him *All. The. Time.*

I PRACTICALLY SPIT mocha out my nose at the dumb-founded look on Q's face when Mira told him she'd had a crush on him for a year. The last week of misery was worth it for that one moment. Priceless.

"Now Mira," I said patiently, trying not to laugh out loud, "go ahead and tell Q how you really feel. Don't hold back."

Mira was so happy it wouldn't have surprised me to see little rainbows floating above her head. She just stared at Q adoringly. It was probably a little scary for him, actually.

"Q?"

His one word question brought every happy thought in my head to a crashing halt. It was like a needle scratching the record to a stop.

"Huh?" I said, my damn cheeks starting to heat up. I did NOT just call him Q to his face.

"Did you just call me '*Q*'?" Kellen's gaze was alarmingly direct, those crazy blue eyes of his suddenly boring into mine. I wanted to shout 'curiosity killed the cat, dude!' but instead, I stuttered…at a complete loss of how to explain my moment of insanity.

"Yes, she said Q," Mira replied matter-of-factly. She was spreading her books out on the table as she talked, seemingly unaware that she was revealing top secret, eyes-only, need-to-know information. "It's our code-name for you. It stands for the Quintessential Quarterback." She said the words with a flare, waving her hands in those ridiculous gloves she loved to wear, like it was some fabulous name that needed no further explanation.

Kellen blinked his eyes over to Mira for a split-second, his brows pulling down in confusion, before they latched onto me again like a pair of x-ray leeches out of some disturbing sci-fi movie.

"Code name?" He said the words slowly, like he was sounding out a foreign language. He tilted his head at me—waiting.

Oh, holy chicken head. I wanted to melt into a pile of complete humiliation and hide under the table. Or have Scotty beam me up to another planet where at least I might have some sort of weapon to fight leech-eyes. I'm pretty sure my face was ready to fry off my body from extreme degrees of embarrassment by now. But when all else fails—plead complete moronic ignorance and turn the question on its head.

"Did I say that?" I asked, all innocent-like. I tilted my head to match his, bravely staring him down, even though I could feel my cheeks radiating heat. I do think, however, the 'prove it' part was convincingly implied. His barely-veiled disbelief melted into something else: surprise. A corner of his mouth twitched. Then his eyes narrowed.

"Ivy." There was a tone in his voice, like maybe he was going to give me a lecture or something. I braced myself. "You didn't tell me you had a personality."

My mouth sagged open at his insult.

Then his lips curved in a smile—a true smile—half of his face complying and the other half twisting in that weird way, and instead of hiding it, he actually laughed. Mira started laughing too.

"Q, you don't know the half of it," she said, like they'd been best friends for years. "Ivy tries to use that blank face thing when she wants, but you know what they say about still waters." Mira tapped her head as she shuffled through her papers looking for some assignment. "That girl is thinking all the time."

She didn't see Q's face shift to that sexy half-grin thing he did with that damn dimple. He raised his eyebrows at me and his x-ray eyes were suddenly making me warm all over.

"Yeah," he said, his gaze never wavering. "I guess I'm going to have to get to know Ivy better."

"THAT WAS FUN!" Mira cried as she shoved Jefferson into gear and spun out of the parking lot.

"Whoa, easy, girl," I yelled, grabbing onto the screamer strap that hung from the ceiling of the car. We were both thrown left as she took a hard right onto the road, then with a squeal of the little tires, we swung back to the middle as she jerked the car into the next gear. "I'd like to stay alive long enough to celebrate your newfound friendship with your obsession."

"He was *nice,* wasn't he?" She flipped her head to look at me, sending her long ponytails flying. I dodged toward the window as the right one almost wapped me in the face. "I *knew* he was nice. He's too good-lucking not to be nice. He couldn't be stuck-up like all those other jocks."

"Yeah, he was much nicer today than normal," I admitted. After my total humiliation, Q actually *had* been nice. And he didn't seem to mind Mira being there at all. In fact, he was much friendlier with her than he'd ever been with me. Like he didn't even care if she saw his lips twist or not. A familiar twinge went through my chest and I shifted positions in my seat. What was with the twinges lately?

"Yeah, he did seem to like to talk to me," Mira chirped. "But, you know—" she flipped her head to look at me again— "he seems like he respects you and all."

Respects me? I guess that was an improvement from the invisibility cloak I'd been wearing last week.

"How are you doing keeping up with your other studies?" Mira continued talking, oblivious to my silence. "That
must be a real shizzle-load. Thank God I'm a drama major—
I couldn't even contemplate doing everything you do. Has
your mom been flippin' out about keeping up with your
homework? And what's the latest with Brandon? Is he still
texting every day?" She gave me a sly grin. "That boy's got
it bad for you."

Mira kept up a steady flow of conversation with herself.
I interjected a few answers here and there to keep her happy
but I wasn't feeling as chatty as she was. I looked out the
window but instead of the trees and neighborhood houses
we were passing, I kept seeing that look on Q's face in study
hall. Mira interrupted my musings. "Are you going to ask
him to Sadie Hawkins? It's next weekend, you know."

"What?" I gasped and jerked around to face her.

"Sa-die Haw-kins. Hello? Earth to Ivy - are you going to
ask Brandon to Sadie Hawkins?" Mira slammed Jefferson
into third gear with only a slight jerk of the clutch. "Hey!
Maybe I should ask Q." Mira grabbed my hand and squealed,
"We could double-date!"

Chapter Twenty

Kellen

I didn't even know what to think about Ivy's friend, Mira. She was just so weird, but she did make me want to laugh—and not always *with* her, if you know what I mean. Oh well. She didn't need to know that.

And that moment with Ivy—I grinned as I remembered the expression on her face when Mira told me they had a code name for me. I laughed again. Ivy Ly had a code name for me? I punched the pillow and bunched it behind my head, grinning. I never would've guessed that one.

I was stretched out on my bed, waiting for my mom to take me to an appointment with Dr. Murdoch. Not that anything much had changed—I still limped when I walked, dragging my right foot, my right hand and arm were still messed up and I didn't even want to think about my face— but I was still anxious to see what the doctor had to say.

Maybe they'd developed some miraculous pill in the last month for Traumatic Brain Injury victims.

MOM AND I checked in and sat down in the waiting room.

"How are things going with your tutor?" she asked as she thumbed through a magazine.

"Fine." I sounded non-committal and wanted it that way. "I think she's like a genius, or something."

"It's awfully nice of her to go with you to all your classes on top of doing her own studies." My mom glanced at the side of my face before she went back to her magazine. "She must be exhausted at the end of the day."

"Hmmm." I mumbled in response. I hadn't really given a lot of thought to what Ivy Ly's life was like.

"Kellen Peterson." The nurse called my name from the open door that led to the back offices. "The doctor will see you now."

We went in and the nurse checked my weight— "you're still down, Kellen" —my blood pressure, pulse and lungs. "Any new problems?"

Like I didn't have enough already? I shook my head.

"How's your memory? Any improvements?"

I shrugged. If my recent quiz results were any indication, that answer would be a definite no. But the truth was, after Ivy had gone over the test with me, I had understood where I'd made my mistakes. And two of the wrong answers had just been simple subtraction errors.

"Okay, Kellen." She snapped the file closed and smiled at me. "The doctor will be in to see you shortly."

I swung my legs as I waited on the elevated bench and tried to open and close my right hand. I hated to even look at those curled up fingers. I couldn't even grip a football. Every day I wrapped my fingers around the ball, carefully positioning them over the strings as if I was going to throw a pass, but I didn't have the strength to grip the ball tightly enough to hold it with my right hand. If I lifted it over my shoulder, the ball squirted free. It was like my arm belonged to someone else's body—definitely not mine.

Dr. Murdoch came in through the door, all bustling efficiency, her stethoscope hanging around her neck. She was probably in her forties with short blond hair. She'd been my pediatrician almost since I was born. She had kids that were just a couple years older than me. She went through the same questions the nurse had, nodding and scratching some additional notes.

"I have a report from your physical therapist." She pulled a piece of paper free from the folder and scanned it through the rainbow framed half-glasses perched on the end of her nose. "He says you're a very hard worker and he expects you to make a full recovery." Her eyes shifted to look at me. "That you just need to allow yourself time to let your body heal and to retrain those muscles."

She stood up and moved over to me, holding the tuning fork or whatever it was that checked reflexes. She checked both my knees and surprisingly my right knee reacted. "Hmmm," she said, straightening up. "That's a good sign." She slid the tuning fork into her pocket and reached for my right hand. "And how's the hand coming along?"

"It's not," I said. I was afraid my voice would crack if I said anything more. My emotions were so weird now. One minute I'd be fine, the next I'd be trying not to cry. Better not to risk it.

She straightened my fingers, bending them this way and that, testing their flexibility and strength. Satisfied with her examination she laid my hand back on my thigh and looked me in the eye. "What about the cognitive? How's school going?"

I sighed and shifted my position so I didn't have to meet her eyes, running my good hand through my hair. "It's tough," I admitted. "I can't remember things very well yet. And some of the math and science concepts are hard to grasp. It's like I just don't get it." Frustration crept into my voice and I stopped talking.

"But you've got a tutor?"

I nodded.

Her eyes narrowed at me, not in a mean way, but in a doctor-thinking way. "Your speech is better."

"Yes, I've noticed that too," my mom said from where she sat in a chair across the room.

Her comment surprised me but I realized she was right. I wasn't slurring anywhere near like I had been.

Dr. Murdoch rested her hand on my shoulder. "Give yourself time, Kellen. You've had a traumatic injury to your brain. It takes a while for that tissue to heal or regenerate." She dropped her hand and stepped back to the file, leaning down to make some notes. "I'd like you to increase your piano practice. New studies are showing that the act of learning and reading music while simultaneously playing with both hands has had dramatic results on cognitive recovery as well as manual dexterity."

She straightened up and faced me. "Try and play two hours a day." She raised her eyebrows and gave me an 'I dare you' look. "Pretend it's football practice." She snapped the file closed and held it to her chest as she walked across to the door. "I'd like to see Kellen back here in another month, Mrs. Peterson."

My mouth was still hanging open when the door snapped shut behind her. Practice piano two hours a day? Was the woman out of her mind?

IN THE LAST month and a half I'd learned that fear and desperation were even more powerful motivators than Coach Branson yelling at me. My mom gave me one of her pep talks on the way home from the doctor's office.

"Why don't you try playing the piano more, Kellen? It won't hurt you to expand your horizons beyond sports a bit." She didn't make a big deal of it. "Dr. Murdoch is very smart. I don't think she'd suggest you play the piano unless she really thought it would help."

"Yeah." I looked out the window as we drove. The streets I used to ride my bike down, the field where we used to play ball in the summer, the road to the lake—all of it looked different now. My perspective on everything had changed. What I'd taken for granted before now seemed like the carrot at the end of a stick I couldn't reach. I guess that's what you get for scrambling your brains. I sighed and let my head fall back against the headrest. "I'll try."

Chapter Twenty-One

Ivy

The next week went by in a blur. Q and I settled into an easier routine with his classes and each other. By now, everybody knew I was his tutor and nobody seemed to think much of it—it was high school—there was always some other new gossip to be spread. Besides, everyone loved him no matter what condition he was in.

At lunch, Q always went to sit with Ollie and CJ and the rest of his jock friends, like we didn't even know each other. I noticed that Jazzy always sat with Ollie though. The one girl in the group of boys. I wondered if that was a sign of true love.

Fourth period I had orchestra and Q went to the gym and did some of his PT exercises, then we'd meet again in the piano room for fifth period. The only person that seemed to be bothered by our tutoring arrangement was Laurel Simmons. I caught the flirty looks she gave him and wondered what her game was. Even though she was dating Josh

99

Hendershot now, it was like she knew she could get Q to dangle on the end of a string for her. Sadly, I wasn't convinced that he wouldn't do it if she asked.

Fifth period piano practice had evolved into its own peculiar routine. It was just the two of us alone in the practice room and Q asked me to play almost every day. He knew, as I did, that nobody would know, or probably care, if we didn't play the piano at all.

"It helps relax me, Ivy," he said in that annoyingly charming way of his. Did anyone ever tell the guy no? I didn't know if he was telling the truth or not, but I agreed to play for ten minutes at the end of the period, but he had to practice the rest of the time.

When I played, he always sat back in his chair and closed his eyes, giving me the opportunity to stare at his near-perfect features. I hated to admit it, but I enjoyed that ten minutes as much as he seemed to.

I DROPPED MY backpack on the table in study hall. It was Wednesday. Midterms were next week and I was feeling the pressure of trying to keep up. Q was already seated with his back to the room, like normal, his books spread out before him.

"Hey." He smiled at me. He was much more relaxed around me now and didn't seem to care if I saw his wonky smile or not. "How are you?"

I looked up in surprise. He was wearing a baseball cap backwards, pulling his hair away from his forehead. I pretended I didn't notice how crazy blue his eyes were. I think it was the first time he'd ever asked about me. I didn't really think before I answered.

"Stressed." I sat down and unzipped my bag.

He was watching me. "Have you always gotten straight A's?"

"Yeah. I didn't have a choice." I pulled my trig book out of my backpack. "My parents would have kicked me out of the house if I didn't."

He was silent for a minute. "You get a lot of pressure from home?" There was something in his voice that made me pause. Like *he* felt sorry for *me*.

"Yes and no." I rested my chin on my hand. "My parents just want the best for me. They know I can do it, so they push me. It was the same for my brother."

"What does he do?" Kellen genuinely seemed interested.

"He's a senior at Columbia University in New York. Pre-med. He's hoping to eventually intern at Johns Hopkins before setting up his residency."

"And what's your life plan, Ivy Ly?" One side of Q's mouth quirked, but I could sense the true curiosity behind the question. "Are you going to go to an Ivy League college and set up your residency somewhere, too?"

I shrugged, wondering why I was telling him all this. "Something like that." I didn't tell him that I couldn't decide between music, medicine or a vapor trail to Paris. I was supposed to have my plan in place by now. "But what about you?" I stared back at him. If he could ask me personal questions, I could ask him, as well. "It can't be easy to be the star quarterback and keep up good grades. You're taking advanced classes and almost carrying a 4.0 too."

He adjusted his hat with his left hand and looked away for a minute. Almost as if he was afraid to admit something. "Yeah. Sometimes it is tough. It's not like my mom and dad have ever said 'do this' or 'accomplish that' or we'll kick you out—" he smiled at me— "but I've grown up with this *expectation*. Like everybody expects me to be the star quarterback—to get picked up by the Pac-12, *and* get good grades. To be Kellen Peterson." His voice held a bitter note. "Whoever that is." He rubbed his forehead like maybe he had a headache.

"I know exactly what you mean." And surprisingly, I meant it. The pressure to be Ivy Ly, the symphony show-case, who would be a world-class surgeon one day was ever-present, every day. To always be taking my playing—and my life—to the next level. To *excel.*

"The weirdest part?" Kellen's face looked so honest and open. In that instant I caught a glimpse behind the 'star quarterback' curtain that he draped himself in and saw the young man turning the wheel to make himself appear big-ger and better than real life. "Now I expect it of myself. Sometimes— " he hesitated and leaned toward me, his voice low enough that only I could hear him— "I'm afraid I'll fail, Ivy. Fail myself. Everybody." A shadow crossed his face. "Especially now."

Something happened to me in that moment. It was a feel-ing I'd never experienced before in my entire life. It was like my heart zinged. And I'm pretty sure that empty place inside me wasn't quite as empty any more.

"What are you two whispering about over here?" Mira swung her black sparkly messenger bag off her shoulder and swung it onto her lap as she sat down. Her hair was dyed entirely black today. It was a bit shocking, actually. Even for me, and I was used to her extreme wardrobe.

"Nothing," I said in my most casual voice, not looking at Q. "Just some homework stuff."

She was wearing a black and red Michael Jackson Thriller t-shirt where he looked like a zombie in mid-dance step, his hands swung up to the side like claws. She was wearing black pants, white socks and black penny loafers to complete the ensemble. Only Mira could pull it off, but I knew for a fact that she could dance Thriller to perfection, because we played the Wii dance version and she killed it every time.

"Well, I'm here to save you," she said. "In honor of it being Thriller day—"

"It's Thriller day?" Q asked with a puzzled look.

"Just in Mira's world." I reassured him.

Mira dug through her bag. "Look what I've got!" She pulled out an entire box of Twinkies and grinned. "Brain food!"

Chapter Twenty-Two

Kellen

I was quiet when my mom picked me up after school to take me to physical therapy. God, were emotional info-dumps a symptom of TBI too? I couldn't believe what I'd revealed to Ivy. Since when did I let *anyone* know I was afraid I might fail? I barely admitted it to myself.

Uncomfortable, I shifted in my seat, but there was no getting away from the truth I'd spilled. It was out there now. I leaned my head back against the head rest and sighed. Hopefully, Ivy would keep it to herself. At least she hadn't said anything to Mira. In front me, anyway. I sighed again. What a train wreck I'd become.

My teeth pulled at my lower lip as I stared out the window and wondered what Ivy's home life was really like. I hadn't had enough time to ask her what she wanted to major in at college. Or where she even wanted to go to college. But

I was sure she had her future mapped out as clearly as her brother's. Surprisingly, I wanted to know the answers.

"Everything okay, honey?" My mom's question broke up my thoughts.

"Yeah. It's fine. I was just thinking about something Ivy said."

"Ivy's your tutor?"

"Yep." I looked at the window again. We were passing the little league fields where I'd grown up playing baseball. I wondered where Ivy marked the years of her childhood. I'd heard she was a tennis player. Was it tennis courts or libraries or performing arts centers?

"Kellen, did you hear me?" My mom poked me in the arm.

I jerked my head around to look at my mom. "Huh?"

"What do you think?" We were stopped at a red light and she was giving me an expectant look.

"About what?"

"About asking Ivy over for dinner as a thank you for all her help." The light changed and we moved forward. "It's a tremendous sacrifice on her part to try to go to your classes and keep up with her own."

I thought about that idea for about two seconds. Today was the first real conversation we'd had since she'd started tutoring me. "Nah, I don't think so, Mom. We're not exactly friends." I readjusted my hat and looked out the window. "Yet," I whispered to my reflection.

Chapter Twenty-Three

Ivy

I n the end, Mira decided it was too soon to ask Q to Sadie Hawkins. I had gently tried to point out that since the guy had trouble walking, I doubted he wanted to try to dance with a stranger. In combat boots. So, she asked Tank Bergstrom instead, who seemed very happy to say yes.

I asked Brandon, Shelby asked Glen Hawkins and Lily asked Ryan Larsen. We decided to all go together, which was going to be interesting. Tank was a metal head, totally into his music, Brandon was an orchestra geek, Glen was a baseball player and friends with Q, and Ryan was a granola boy but I secretly thought he was a closet pothead. I hadn't mentioned that to Lily though. But we'd all known each other for the last four years, some of us longer, so I figured it would be fine.

The theme for Sadie Hawkin's was "Celebrity Night." Brandon and I decided to go as Pierce Brosnan and Renee Russo from The Thomas Crowne Affair. That way he could wear his orchestra tux and I could take another stab at wearing a fancy dress. I was pretty sure no one would recognize which celebrities we were, but it would still be fun to pretend we were über-rich. And Mira had a short red wig I could borrow and a ton of costume jewelry. Hopefully, no one would puke on me.

The four of us planned to get ready at The Mansion. I was the first to arrive and ran up the grand staircase to Mira's room. She was going as Lady Gaga and Tank was going to be her lead guitarist. Hardly a stretch for either of them. Mira was sitting in front of her big white vanity, the one from Pottery Barn, putting on some outrageous makeup when I got there.

"Nice boots." I motioned to her hot pink combat boots. She was wearing a super short dress that revealed a lot of leg. "What are you going to wear with them?"

"Ha ha, very funny," Mira said, not even pausing in her application of fake eyelashes. A hot pink lightning bolt colored one whole side of her face.

"Lucky thing you have good legs," I said. "Tank's going to like that outfit."

Mira grinned at me over her shoulder. "Too bad Q's not going to see me."

I laughed. "Probably better he's not. You'd probably give him a heart attack."

Mira stuck her finger in her mouth then touched it to her hip. 'Siiizzzzzz. Too hot to handle."

I rolled my eyes and snorted. "Whatever."

She shooed me with her hand. "Get your dress on. Shelby and Lily are going to be here any minute."

I pulled my dress from the garment bag.

"Ohhhh, that's pretty," Mira said.

It was a dress I had worn for a few piano showcases. Black and glittering, it was tight enough to show off my slim figure, and hit me just above the knees. Plus, I had a great pair of black heels that went with it. Elegant but sexy, sort of like one of the dresses Renee Russo had worn in the movie – this one just wasn't see-through like hers had been. Thankfully.

Shelby and Lily arrived a few moments later. Glen was going as Edgar Martinez, a retired Mariners baseball player (big surprise) so Shelby decided to dress up as a cheerleader. Somehow she'd found a real cheerleader outfit on Ebay that actually fit.

Ryan was going as John Lennon so Lily opted for Yoko, which was a little bit funny as I was the only Asian in the crowd, but she found a wig and some big glasses and the most God-awful bell bottoms.

Glen picked us up in his mom's huge SUV so all eight of us could fit in the car.

"Scoot over," I giggled as Lily half-sat on me and wapped me in the face with her Yoko Ono hair.

"Mira's shoving me!" Lily laughed, her big white glasses sliding down her nose while she tried to shove back as we crammed into the far back seat. "Don't step on my toes with those boots!"

Shelby got to ride shotgun because Glen was her date. Brandon, Ryan and Tank somehow got stuck sitting together but they managed to squeeze into the middle seat with less drama than the three of us in the back. After about ten minutes of squirming and adjusting we finally headed to the school. As we were driving out of Springwood, Glen tooted his horn at somebody on the sidewalk. I peered out the window, squinting to see through the settling dark as we drove past. I froze as I recognized broad shoulders. Was that Q?

The guy raised his left hand at Glen. It looked like he was holding a football. Did Q live around here? For a second, I thought he saw me through the glass. His head swiveled to follow the car's passage and he seemed to be looking right at my window.

Giggles and laughter filled the car around me, for but for a second it was like I was standing alone on that corner watching the car full of laughing kids drive by. I leaned forward and pressed my nose against the glass, watching him until we turned the corner and he was out of sight.

"Ivy, what are you doing?" Mira asked.

I jerked my head back, suddenly aware of how I must look. "Nothing. I thought I saw something… weird out there."

"Weird, like in what? A ghost?" Brandon asked.

His comment was oddly appropriate. It was like Q was a ghost of himself anymore.

But that was all it took to get the car laughing again. By the time we got to the school, I'd forgotten all about Q.

Almost.

THE NIGHT WAS nearly over and the band was taking their last break, so for the moment we could actually hear ourselves. We sat around a big circular table talking and drinking the lame lemonadey kind of punch stuff they had.

Two tables over Laurel Simmons was all over Josh Hendershot. Her hair was messed up, her lipstick was smeared and it was only by a miracle that any part of her boobs were still covered by the low cut top she kept pushing in Josh's face. I was pretty sure they'd had more than lemons in their lemonade.

"Who do you suppose they are," Mira whispered in my ear as she nodded in their direction. "Courtney Love and her dealer?"

I laughed under my breath. "Mrrreoww. Vicious when you want to be, aren't you?"

"It's not like she doesn't deserve it."

"Hey, did you hear about Paris?" Brandon asked, nudging me with his elbow. He really looked cute tonight, in his tux and with his hair all fashionably spiked. He had such a friendly face and easy smile. He never made me nervous.

"No." My curiosity bubbled over. "Paris who?"

"What's this about Paris?" Mira leaned closer. She was as Paris-crazy as I was. We daydreamed about living there one day and talked about how when we fell in love we'd put a padlock on one of the bridges as a sign of our undying love.

"Oh, that's right," he said, looking at me, "you weren't there. You were gone tutoring." There was no inflection in his words. In fact, he didn't seem bothered by my tutoring Kellen Peterson at all. "Mr. Flynn announced on Friday that Heritage Festivals is putting on an international orchestra competition in Paris over spring break. If they can get enough kids to commit, he'll chaperone a group of us there to compete."

My mouth dropped open. Paris in the spring. It would be my dream come true.

WE DROPPED LILY and Ryan off first. When Glen dropped me off, Brandon got out of the car and gallantly walked me to the front porch.

"Thanks for asking me, Ivy," he said, his arm on my elbow. "That was really fun tonight."

"Yeah, thanks for coming." I turned to face him. "I had a blast." And it was true. I'd had a great time. We'd laughed all evening and even though we were all so different, the dance had been a lot of fun.

Brandon stepped onto the porch step next to me and moved closer. My heart started racing. We were standing directly under the porch light and part of my brain wondered if he was going to kiss me while the other half wondered if Mira and the guys were watching from the car.

Somebody rolled a window down and I heard them giggling. Suddenly Tank yelled, "kiss her!"

Before Brandon could see me blush he leaned forward and pressed his lips to mine. I pressed back. So this is kissing, I thought. Big deal. Then it was over.

Glen started honking the horn and Brandon stepped back, looking pleased with himself. On the other side of the door, I could hear my father's measured footsteps approach. I widened my eyes at Brandon and he stepped away.

"Okay, see you later," I said, just as my father opened the front door.

"Ivy, what's all the commotion out here? It's after midnight. The neighbors are trying to sleep."

"Hello Mr. Ly." Brandon reached forward and shook my father's hand. "Thanks for letting Ivy come out with me tonight."

"Oh, hello Brandon." My father gave him a little half-bow. He was old-school—some things never change. At least Brandon totally got it. "Be careful driving home."

"Yes, sir." Brandon grinned at me and then ran back to the car.

"Bye Ivy," Mira called out the window, waving.

I rested my hand on the knob of the front door and waved back. She was probably more excited about my first kiss than I was. At least they'd had enough sense to stop honking the horn.

Chapter Twenty-Four

Kellen

I got to fifth period early on Monday, before Ivy arrived. I'd spent a lot of time working on the piano lately, struggling to read the notes on the page, to get my fingers to go where my brain told them to go. But things actually seemed to be improving.

I pulled the intermediate piano book I was working from out of my backpack and stood it up on the stand. It always took a few minutes for the fingers on my right hand to warm up so I started working on a simple C scale. Though I had taken piano lessons for four years when I was younger, I hadn't played once in the three years since I'd quit. Now after my brain injury, I wasn't sure there was anything left to remember.

After a few minutes my fingers felt looser so I started the song on the page. I played just my left hand for a few measures, trying to get the rhythm of the repeating phrases so I wouldn't have to think so much about that hand when I tried to add in the right hand.

It took a few minutes before I got a nice rhythm going with my left hand but every time I tried to come in with my right hand, I got jumbled up.

"Dammit." I swore under my breath, my shoulders starting to tense up.

"Here."

Ivy's voice was so close to my ear I jumped. "Shit." I faked a cough and cleared my throat. "Sorry. I didn't know you were back there."

She smiled at me—soft and—different.

"I can be sneaky like that sometimes. I get it from my mother." She leaned close to my right side and placed her small hand on top of my right hand. "Let me help you." Her long dark hair slid off her right shoulder as she moved and the fragrant scent of plumeria wafted around my head. Fifth period was definitely the best part of my day.

She pressed down on my spastic fingers to make them play the keys. She didn't even seem to notice that they were so messed up.

"Keep your fingers relaxed and your wrists straight. You don't have to rush." With her help, suddenly the notes sounded like music instead of torture by piano. "There." She tilted her head to look at me. "Can you feel the difference?"

She was so close I could see how perfect her skin was and the delicate black lashes that framed her dark eyes. I wondered what she was thinking at the same time I thought about kissing her.

It was like she read my mind because all of a sudden she jerked her head back and hurried to sit in the chair. "Keep playing," she said over her shoulder. "You're doing great."

I turned back to the piano, a sick feeling twisting in my gut. What the hell was I thinking? Kissing my tutor? Not only was that totally wrong and the most stupid thing I could think to do, but I knew she had a boyfriend.

Self-loathing was my new best friend. Two months ago I probably could have dated any girl in this school. Now I probably couldn't get a date—and to make matters worse—I wanted to hit on my tutor, the one person I should probably never date. God, I was such a loser.

Chapter Twenty-Five

Ivy

When I got home from school I went directly to my room. I flopped on my back onto the bed and left my feet hanging over the edge. I put one of the orange throw pillows over my face and screamed "HOLY CHICKEN HEAD" into it. What was wrong with me? This afternoon in fifth period, when I was helping Q play the treble notes with his right hand, I had thought about kissing him. KISSING HIM!

I groaned in utter mortification. The truth was I had *wanted* to kiss him. But I was his tutor! Tutor's don't kiss their students. Even if they are the most beautiful ex-football playing boys that have ever walked the face of the earth. That's like sexual harassment or something. I'd probably get arrested if anybody knew, not to mention that I sort-of have a boyfriend and the very most important part: Q WAS MY BEST FRIEND'S *OBSESSION*.

"Ivy?" I jerked the pillow off my face at the sound of my mother's voice. Sneaky, that woman. Her head was poked around the corner of the door jamb and she was staring at me with a confused frown. "Is everything all right? I thought I heard you scream."

"No— I mean yeah—Ma. Everything's fine. I was … er…singing."

My mom scrunched her eyebrows like she didn't believe me.

"What are you doing home?"

She brushed a wave of gray-streaked hair off her forehead. "We had a furlough day at work today. Don't forget Dr. Cobbs wants you to start working on the Christmas pieces for the Youth Symphony."

"I've been working on 'em, Ma." I pushed off the bed and went over to grab my laptop off my desk. "I've got some other homework to do first." Which was totally the truth. I was putting in long hours, up until midnight every night, trying to keep up with the homework from my regular classes.

"Mrs. Chang told me that Brandon has applied to the San Francisco Conservatory of Music." There was a disapproving note in her voice. "He could be a doctor if he wanted." She hovered in the doorway, waiting for my reaction.

I smiled at my mother, giving no indication that I might like to apply there too. "I hope he gets in, I think he'd love it there." The sing-song tone of an incoming Skype call rang on my laptop. "I've gotta get this, ma." I clicked on "Answer with video" and Mira's face popped up.

"Hey!" she chirped.

"Don't forget to practice your piano," my mother muttered as she disappeared back downstairs.

I shut my bedroom door and plunked down on my bed with my computer on my lap.

"I think Q was flirting with me in study hall today, don't you?" Mira said as she painted her fingernails black.

"Yeah, I think he was too." And I did. After my insane moment at the piano, Q had barely looked at me the rest of the day. Had he somehow known what I'd been thinking? Instead of staying over after school for a few minutes, like we sometimes did, he bolted right at the bell. Whatever. I was happy for Mira that she and Q were becoming such good friends. I was.

Ugh. I had to stop thinking about him. "Have you heard from Tank?" I asked.

"Oh yeah. He texts me all the time. Wants me to go to one of his gigs this weekend, but I don't know." She looked into the camera. "I don't want people to think I'm his groupie or something."

I laughed. Mira was too original to be somebody's groupie. "I wouldn't worry. Where's he playing at?"

"Oh, they've got something going on down at The Crypt." She paused to blow on her outstretched fingers. "But that place is a little scary."

"Ya think?" I snorted. "They just busted some guys down there for meth a couple of weeks ago and don't you remember last summer when somebody got stabbed in the parking lot?" I shook my head, even though she wasn't looking at me. "That place is bad news. You're not thinking of going, are you?"

Mira shrugged. "No, not really. What's up with Brandon?" She disappeared from the screen and I could hear her rattling around in the background.

"He's going to some weekend cello camp in Seattle. But it doesn't matter because I've got homework anyway." I groaned. "Tons and tons of homework. Plus I haven't practiced near enough on my piano." I glanced at the door to make sure it was shut. I didn't want my mother to hear that last comment.

Mira popped back into the picture. "Q seems like he's getting better, doesn't he?" Now she was looking directly at me. "How much longer do you think you'll get to tutor him?"

Mr. Decker had never given me a timeframe, probably because nobody knew how quickly he'd recover. But I could definitely see improvement. Q's speech was better and his memory seemed to be improving.

"Probably just until he gets caught up in his classes. Maybe 'til Christmas break. Maybe January." I shrugged, but a little voice in the back of my head squeaked 'or February, please'. "I don't know. Why?"

Mira pushed her face really close to the camera and spoke in a furtive whisper. "I want to know how long I have to slip him the magic love potion." Then she laughed and sat back, and spoke in her normal voice. "Because you know perfectly well, once he doesn't need you anymore, he won't be hanging out with us."

That's what I loved best about Mira. She just said it the way it was. Didn't get in a big huff about anything. Like being used for your brains.

I smiled at her. "Well, if today was any indication, I'd say it's starting to work."

Mira took a big bite of a Twinkie and smiled at me, her teeth all full of yellow sponge cake and cream. "I knouwf."

I stared at the blank screen for a long time after Mira disconnected. What was I doing? Mira had liked Q for over a year. It didn't matter that he hadn't even known she was alive until a few weeks ago. That didn't change how she felt about him. Which meant I *couldn't* feel that way about him. And who knows? Maybe he felt the same way about her. People change. Up until a few weeks ago I had thought all football players were stupid jocks who only cared about winning.

I thought of Brandon and how cute he was and such a good, nice person. He always had a smile on his face and worked so hard to excel in school, partly I know, just to make his parents proud. We'd been friends forever and now he *like* liked me. I couldn't waste one more second thinking about Q and things that could never be. Besides, we weren't really even friends. He was only around so I could help him catch up on his studies. I was his tutor, he was my student. I wouldn't *allow* myself to think of him in other way.

Chapter Twenty-Six

Kellen

Tomorrow was Thanksgiving break. I could hardly wait. Football season was officially over. The Eagles had ended with a 6-3 record. They'd made it to post-season play but been eliminated in the first game. Somehow I felt twenty pounds lighter. Well, I *was* twenty pounds lighter, but you know what I mean. A huge sense of relief filled me at not having to face the weekly games and stand on the sidelines to watch Carter play my position. Now I could focus my energy on other things.

Since my moment of insanity when I'd thought about kissing Ivy a few weeks ago I'd worked really hard to be cool around her. The last thing I needed was to freak her out and make her think I was into her as a person. Even if I did think about her way more often than was normal. What would Ivy think about this? Would Ivy like that? It was weird. She was my super-brained tutor. That was it.

"Hey Peterson, let's go." Ollie called to me from across the hall. Most of the kids at school treated me exactly the same as they always had. Like they thought I was cool. Maybe it was just because I was tall, but they still acted like I was the star quarterback half the time. Everybody that is, except Laurel. She was hard to figure. She'd smile at me now, in that sexy way she had, so at least she knew I was alive, but she never talked to me or made an effort to hang around my friends. She was all into Josh now. Even though he was a little rodent.

I raised my hands at Ollie. "What?" We were in the crowded hallway between third and fourth period just headed to lunch.

"Let's ditch this popsicle stand. They're not gonna miss us for three periods." He motioned for me with his hand. "C'mon."

I hesitated. I wouldn't see Ivy in fourth period but I felt like I should let her know I wasn't going to be there for piano and study hall. And to tell her to have a nice holiday.

"Dude." CJ appeared at my elbow. He must have been behind me in the hall. "What is the holdup? Let's go now while we can get out without being seen."

"I should let Ivy know I'm leaving."

CJ tilted his head back and made a face. "What is she? Your mommy?"

"No, but—"

He grabbed my arm and started shoving me through the crowd. "Text her, man. She'll get the message."

'Yeah, okay." We ditched our books in our lockers and headed out the back door of Hall Four to the side parking lot where Ollie had his black Nissan parked. It felt great to be sneaking out. Like I was normal again.

CJ climbed in the back, since I had the gimp leg and all, and I rode in the front with Ollie. As soon as I sat down I pulled my phone out to text Ivy.

"What? You got the hots for this girl or somethin'?" CJ asked. He was sitting forward with his head between the two front seats. "Cuz you're sure acting like you're whipped."

Ollie laughed as he fired up the engine. "I thought Peterson was still hung up on Laurel Simmons." The music immediately started blasting, the low bass notes pounding out a rhythm that shook the car. "I heard she and Josh are on the outs," he yelled over the music.

"Dude, turn it down, would ya?" I stared at my phone, suddenly realizing I didn't have Ivy's cell number. Shit. How had I not thought to ask her for it after all this time?

"It's okay, Kell." CJ laughed and punched Ollie in the shoulder. "I get where you're coming from. Your tutor's pretty fine to look at. It's just all those brains that would scare me."

"Yeah, yeah, whatever." I scrolled through my contacts list. CJ might be a standout wide receiver but academics were never his interest. He lived to play ball. Suddenly I stopped in the M's. I had Mira's number. She'd given it to me in study hall the first time I'd met her. I could still remember what she said when she handed me the slip of paper: *'In case you need somebody to talk to.'* I'd smiled and said 'okay, thanks' at the time. Like I'd call goofy Mira if I needed someone to talk to. But right now, I was really glad I had her number.

I sent her a text: *Hey Mira, it's Kellen. I had to leave early today. Can you let Ivy know?* I punched send, feeling a lot better. There. I'd told her. There was no reason for her to be pissed. Then I sent a second message: *Hv a good break.* I shoved my phone into my back pocket with a sigh of relief. I was free for four days.

WE ENDED UP hanging at Ollie's house. He had a great Xbox 360 set-up in their basement and both of his parents worked. Nobody would know we'd cut class. I'd practiced enough at home with a joystick that I could at least hold my own again in a game of Halo. It felt like it had been forever since I'd just hung out with my friends.

"So what's the latest with Jazzy?" I asked Ollie. I was stretched out in one of the recliner portions of their big brown leather couch. CJ was in the other one, with Ollie on the floor leaning back against the couch in the middle. The shades were pulled and the room was dark, lit only by one lamp and the glow of the 65" TV. "Any marriage plans yet?" I joked.

Ollie and Jazzy had been going out since the beginning of their sophomore year. I didn't think either of them had dated anyone else. We called them the old married couple. At least they didn't make out in the halls all the time like they used to the first year they went out.

"What's Jazzy gonna do when you go play college ball?" CJ asked, as he jerked his joystick to shoot somebody. "Damn! Missed him."

"Jazzy's applying to colleges too, isn't she?" I asked as I missed three easy shots and took a bullet to the heart. Shit. "I mean, you don't know if you're going to end up at the same school, right?"

"Yeah." Ollie said. "I don't know." Something in his tone made me glance over at him.

"What?"

Ollie had a sick look on his face. "Jazzy's pregnant."

Chapter Twenty-Seven

Ivy

Mira told me at lunch that she'd gotten a text from Q. I didn't even ask how he had her cell number. He'd never asked me for mine.

"Good," I said, munching on a piece of celery like I could care less. "I need to practice my piano piece for the Christmas concert anyway."

"What are you doing over Thanksgiving?" Mira asked. She was the Union Jack today. Her entire shirt looked like a replica of the British flag and her skinny leg pants were red. Her hair had streaks of blue and she wore white fingerless gloves, which very nicely showcased fingernails painted like the Union Jack too. I wondered how long that had taken her. Possibly an entire episode of Ellen.

In contrast, I wore jeans and a black sweater. It was all about balance. "We're going to my uncle's. You know Vietnamese families—lots of relatives. What about you?"

"Staying home. My grandma's coming over. Want to do something on Friday?" She was eating a Twinkie. As her main dish.

"Yep. Call me." We headed our different directions for fourth period. Since Q was gone, I decided to practice my own piano pieces during fifth period. It was a little weird being there without him—at first I kept expecting him to walk in, but after I started playing I forgot about him. The piece I was playing for the showcase was complicated and I was still working on memorizing part of it. I had to repeat some passages over and over. Almost thirty minutes had passed when I finished with a flourish.

Someone starting clapping behind me. Surprised, I turned to see who it was.

Brandon stood leaning against the door jamb. "You're amazing, Ivy." He stood up and walked toward me. "Your playing is so effortless. You're going to have colleges beating down the door to get you."

I laughed, pleased with his compliment. "I wish."

He stopped next to the bench and look at the empty chair behind the pillar. "Where's Kellen Peterson today?"

I shrugged. "He had an appointment or something. Which is great," I added in a hurry. "I needed some time to practice."

Brandon nodded. He looked like he was going to say something then he seemed to change his mind. "Want to go boarding over the weekend?"

I perked up. I loved to snowboard. The snow had come early this year and the ski resorts were open for the Thanksgiving weekend. "Sure." Then I sobered. Could I give up an entire day of studying to go to the mountains for fun?

As if reading my mind, Brandon said, "C'mon Ivy, we're only young once."

I laughed. "You're right. Which day are we going?"

THE FOUR DAY WEEKEND flew by. Between cooking for and celebrating Thanksgiving, catching up on homework and music practice, and going snowboarding with Brandon, I hardly thought about Q at all. Which was a huge relief. I didn't want to think about him. Even Mira took a break from talking about him, for which I was very grateful. By the time Monday rolled around I'd put our relationship back into a healthy context again. Whatever my momentarily flight of fancy had been about the guy—it was gone.

I WAS ALREADY seated in first period when Q got to class on Monday. By now, the other kids always left a seat open next to me for him and vice versa. I smiled at him when he slid into the seat about five seconds before the tardy bell was going to ring. He always made it to class with barely seconds to spare.

"Nice timing," I whispered. It only took about two seconds for his physical presence to blow my hair back. Sweet shizzle sauce that guy was good-looking.

He wore a tight black Nike zip-up jacket that showed off his broad shoulders and muscular arms. His blondy-brown hair still looked a bit damp, like he'd showered fifteen minutes before he ran out the door. The ends twisted in little wavy curls that most girls paid a ton of money to get. The cut of his jaw was the stuff that made movie stars famous and dark lashes fringed his magnetic blue eyes. The whole package added up to beautiful. But there was something different about him today that I couldn't put my finger on. Was it that he looked more rested? Then I realized what it was: Q looked happy.

Class hadn't formally started as Mrs. Cooper, the Calculus teacher, was still messing around with some papers at the front of the class.

Q leaned across the aisle to talk to me. That was new. "How was your break?"

I nodded. "Good."

His elbow rested on the desk and he turned sideways in the seat so he could face me. "Sorry I bailed on Wednesday. I had a friend who needed some help. Did you get my message?"

I blinked. Wow. He was a Chatty Kathy this morning. Must've had a strong cup of joe for breakfast. "You mean the one you sent Mira?" I replied. My voice sounded drier than I intended.

"Yeah, well— " for a second he actually looked embarrassed— "I didn't have your cell number. She told you though, right?" He smiled at me, not caring about the wacky side of his mouth. He seemed so *earnest*, I didn't really know what to think. "And did she tell you that I said to have a nice break?"

Mira hadn't told me that part. I was trying to decide if he was joking or not when he kept talking.

"So, can I get your cell number now? You know— " he gave me the sexy half-grin and raised his eyebrows at me— "for emergency purposes?"

My heart skipped a beat. This kind of behavior from Q was not in my healthy context plan. What sort of defense does any girl have against innate charm? Especially in the form of the once-star quarterback? I rattled off my cell number and I'll be damned if he didn't enter it into his phone right then. Mrs. Cooper started the class, but that didn't slow Q down at all. At least he slid around to face forward in his seat, but he turned his head toward me and kept talking.

"Do you want mine?" he whispered.

Was he serious? I quickly reviewed the rules of engagement when one is flustered and buying time to think: Feign ignorance and repeat the question. "Your what?"

"My cell number." He sounded a bit exasperated. "Here." Before I could stop him, he grabbed my hand, turned it over and wrote his cell number in black ink on my palm. 952-6548. Even though I only looked at the numbers for a few seconds I swear they were burned into my brain for eternity.

"Mr. Peterson, do you have a question?" Mrs. Cooper was glaring at us.

He straightened up and smiled, capping his pen with a snap. "No Ma'm. Ivy did." I gasp-snorted and made a face. "But I answered it for her." He grinned at me like a little boy.

"That was very kind of you," Mrs. Cooper said in a voice that didn't sound like she thought he was kind at all. "In the future, Miss Ly, please direct your questions to me." She turned and went back to the board. I debated about pointing out that I had already passed this stupid class but I knew she wouldn't care.

"Funny." I mouthed the word at Q.

He just smiled at me and then pulled out a notebook and started taking his own notes. Up until now, he'd let me take the notes. He peeked out of the corner of his eyes to see if I'd noticed. I raised my eyebrows at his right hand, awkwardly clutching the pen, and nodded in approval.

TEN MINUTES LATER my phone vibrated in my pocket. Mira and I often texted each other during the day. I pulled it out to see what she had to say. But the text wasn't from Mira. It was from Q.

Want to go get coffee after school today?

Chapter Twenty-Eight

Kellen

On one hand, Ollie's news was a shock. On the other hand, it wasn't a surprise at all. Ollie and Jazzy had been doin' it for over two years now. I would've thought they'd got the contraception thing figured out, but Ollie said he never thought one time without protection would make any difference. *One freakin' time.*

I really felt for the guy. For the first time in a long time, I felt sorry for someone besides myself. With my TBI I'd stood on the cliffs of hell and watched my football career disappear in the fiery abyss. But at least for me, there was a chance I could recover. Even if my arm and leg didn't get any better, I could still go to college, party, travel the world—whatever.

For Ollie—the dude just did a swan dive into the flames. Pretty hard to do anything but work your ass off for the rest of your life with a wife and kid to support. Assuming he got married and Jazzy had the baby. He hadn't really said what their plans were. And how far would he get without a college degree? Plus, he was a gifted football player. It had been his dream to play college ball as much as it'd been mine.

I thought a lot about Ollie and life over the four day weekend. About what I wanted to achieve, about what was important to me. And who I wanted to be.

"SO, HOW ABOUT IT?" I asked Ivy as we left first period. "You didn't answer my text. Want to go get coffee after school? The Java Hut has these new mini donuts with chocolate sprinkles that are killer." Ivy walked slowly enough so my limp was hardly noticeable. I realized for the first time that she did it on purpose, though she'd probably never admit it. She was so tiny she barely reached my shoulder. I had a strange urge to put my arm around her and help her navigate the crowded hallway. Not that she needed my help. "Plus, we could work on that science project."

She didn't look at me. Instead she held her books to her chest and stared straight ahead. "That sounds fun, but Mira always gives me a ride home after school."

I thought about that for a minute. "Great! Maybe Mira could come too?" I had to pause and turn sideways to fit my shoulders through the crush of kids. I got caught in the flow as Ivy kept moving forward, forcing me to hop-skip to catch up. I laughed. "Especially since she's the only one with a car. I still haven't got the okay to drive."

Ivy turned and looked up at me, her face perfectly blank. Her black eyes were shadowed by silver-grey makeup. Her lips were the color of crushed cranberries against her tan skin. She was fragile and perfect. The thought of kissing her flitted through my head again. I grinned. God – what a scene that would cause.

Ivy raised her eyebrows. "Why don't you ask her?"

I got the funny feeling something was wrong, but I wasn't sure what it could be. "Good idea. I'll text her."

"Good idea."

WE DIDN'T GET a chance to talk in science. Mr. Pruitt was a dick—it wasn't worth trying to mess with him. But Mira responded to my text with lots of exclamation points after her 'yes' and one of those little smiley-face things that looked like it was blowing a kiss. I moved my phone closer to my face and squinted at the little picture then moved it farther away. Whatever. I gave Ivy a thumbs up to let her know Mira's answer. She just nodded and smiled.

Third period was French, which Mira had too. I don't remember ever seeing her in my class before Ivy started tutoring me, but apparently she'd always been there. It seemed impossible that I could have missed her with all those crazy outfits she wore but apparently I had.

The three of us sat together now and lately Tank Bergstrom had been hanging around too. I didn't really know the guy, other than he was a total head and was really into his music. But he seemed nice enough and he definitely got the material better than I did at this point. Would my brain ever be normal again?

I HAD BEEN practicing hard on the piano and it was finally beginning to show. My fingers were starting to work better and I was remembering the notes easier. Four years of lessons had to have formed some kind of synapses in my brain, right? Ivy seemed pleased with my progress and was very encouraging.

"That's excellent, Q! I can tell how much you've been practicing. It's really paying off, you're doing great."

You'd think I'd get tired of hearing it—but I didn't. I loved it. Especially coming from her, because I don't think she'd pay me a compliment unless she meant it. It was weird, but it made me want to try harder—just to make her proud of me.

When there was only fifteen minutes left in the period I got up and motioned for her to sit on the piano bench. "Your turn."

She waved me off like she wasn't going to play as I worked my gimpy self out from behind the piano.

"Forget it, Ivy. You promised." Before she could move I slipped my hands under her arms and picked her up. She half-shrieked in surprise. She couldn't have weighed more than a hundred and ten. My right arm didn't hold up quite as well as my left, but it was enough to get her over to the bench. I sort-of dropped her in place, then leaned forward to speak in her ear. "A deal's a deal."

She was laughing as she turned toward me. "Okay, okay." Suddenly, we were in a reversal of that moment a few weeks before: Faces frozen, inches apart. Though it was oddly the same, everything was different. *I* was different.

Her lips were partly open and I leaned forward before I could talk myself out it. I felt her warm breath before I crushed my lips to hers. I slipped my hand behind her head, the silky strands of her hair pouring through my fingers like liquid black gold. Her lips were as sweet and tantalizing as the scent of plumeria that I always seemed to smell when I was around her. I kissed her in a way that didn't leave any doubt about how I felt. And damn if she didn't kiss me back.

I pulled back. "Okay?" I asked softly.

She nodded, her lips still parted, tempting me, but her eyes were wide and shocked. "Okay," she whispered.

I sat down in my chair and she hurriedly swung around to face the piano. It was the first time I'd ever heard Ivy mess up a note while she was playing. Her cheeks stayed pink for the rest of the class and it was obvious she was avoiding looking at me. It made me want to laugh out loud and pump my fist in the air. The last time I'd felt like this was when I'd thrown that floating pass to Dillon to win the Homecoming Dance. I hadn't believed I could ever feel like this again.

OLLIE USUALLY GAVE me a ride home after school. When I told him I was going to go study at the Java Hut with Ivy and Mira he just gave me that slow nod and a fist bump. "Cool."

A couple of guys were throwing a football around the parking lot when we walked out to Mira's car. A pang went through me as I watched the football sail past my head. I could've easily reached my left hand up and caught it. It was the throw back that would've been a problem.

"Jefferson's over here," Mira chirped.

"You named your car?" I asked, though with Mira it really would have been more surprising if she *hadn't* named her car.

"Jefferson Christopher Beetle." Ivy and Mira said it at the same time and started laughing. I liked being with Ivy when she was around Mira. It was like getting a glimpse into her secret world. I was surprised to find that I wanted my own personal key.

Luckily, Ivy climbed in the miniature back seat while I tried to cram myself into the miniature front seat. I swear my head was brushing the ceiling. Mira started the engine—which sounded like a little wind-up toy—and jerked the car so bad when she shifted into second gear that I bumped my head against the window.

"Sorry about that," she said, giving me a guilty look. "I have a little trouble with the clutch when I'm shifting." I glanced behind me. Ivy was collapsed on her side in a fit of giggles in the back seat. I'd never heard her laugh so hard.

"Yeah. Thanks for the warning." I reached for the screamer strap and braced myself. Damn. I was definitely going to have to work on getting my parents to let me have my truck back.

Chapter Twenty-Nine

Ivy

I was a bundle of nerves at the Java Hut. I was trying to be cool, no big deal, but every time I looked up Q was watching me with those crazy blues. I tried to pretend the kiss hadn't happened but instant replay was on a constant loop in my head. The sweet taste of cherry coke, the way his lips had covered mine, like he couldn't help himself; the feel of his fingers threaded through my hair, so gentle, pulling me closer. I'd been definitely been kissed and sadly, I loved it. Then I'd look at Mira and guilt practically squeezed the air out of my lungs.

MIRA DROPPED ME OFF first after the Java Hut, as it turned out Kellen lived in Springwood too. So it had been him standing on the corner the night of Sadie Hawkins. I knew Mira would Skype me as soon as she got home to talk about Q, but I couldn't do it. I needed time alone to process. To figure out what I was going to do.

My mother wasn't home from work yet so I dropped my backpack on the floor by the kitchen table and ran upstairs to my room. I threw myself on the bed and buried my face in the pile of colorful pillows. Sliding my arms around their silky fabric, I kicked my legs and screamed. HE KISSED ME!

I so totally wasn't expecting it that when he'd leaned forward and pressed his lips against mine, it had taken me a second to react. But then it had been like a flood of sensations had swallowed me. His lips were so soft, yet demanding, just like they said in all those terrible romance novels. When he'd put his hand in my hair and crushed his lips against mine—I *had* to kiss him back. I *wanted* to kiss him back. So many things I'd never felt before poured through me, filling me up so full—yet making me hungry for more. I was so confused.

Now I knew what it meant to be kissed. Really kissed. I thought of when Brandon had pressed his lips against mine and I started giggling. Two kisses couldn't be farther apart. The next thing I knew I was crying. Why had Q kissed me? Mira had dibs on him and I liked Brandon, *didn't I?*

I rolled over and covered my face with my hands and sobbed like a little girl with a broken heart.

BY EVENING I'D gotten it together again. I didn't know why Q kissed me but we were just friends. It wouldn't happen again. He texted me that night about some inconsequential thing in math. I debated about not answering but decided it would be childish to ignore him. I sent him a quick reply then told him I had to go some place with my parents and I'd see him tomorrow. I could just be friends with him. Everything would be fine.

THE DAY AFTER 'The Kiss' I made a point of mention-ing Brandon a few times during study hall. Mira was gone to a drama meeting about a play they were putting on and it was just Q and me at our table.

He had his math book open and was working on the assignment while I worked on my trig homework.

"I guess Brandon applied to the San Francisco Conservatory," I said, like I thought Q might find that to be a fascinating bit of news. What a joke. The guy probably didn't even know who Brandon Chang was.

Q paused and lifted his head. "The cello guy?"

I blinked in surprise. "Yeah."

He chewed on the end of his pencil while he stared at me with an inscrutable expression. I tried to ignore him but finally I couldn't take it anymore. I put my pencil down and stared back.

"Okay, what?"

"Have you been going out with him for a while?"

My mouth opened and closed a few times like a fish out of water. "I..I've known him a long time," I finally stuttered.

"That wasn't what I asked, Ivy."

My cheeks started to heat up. "Uh, no." I couldn't lie. "Not really."

Q's lips quirked in a lazy grin. "Good." Then he went back to work on his math.

I wanted to ask him what that meant but I didn't dare. The rest of study hall Q was his normal friendly self. He acted like the kiss had never happened at all. I wasn't totally sure how I felt about that.

THAT NIGHT Q called me. I stared at the phone as it buzzed in my hand debating what the correct course of action would be: Take the call and acknowledge our friendship, which really meant I might be acknowledging what was happening behind the scenes, or ignore it and hide like the chicken shit I was.

"Hello?" I couldn't help myself.

"Hey Ivy." His voice sounded lower on the phone. "Sorry to bother you after school but I wondered if you could help me for a few minutes on these French translations. They're kickin' my butt." He sounded really tired.

"Did you go to physical therapy today?" I don't know where that came from, but I did want to know. I felt sorry for him. He worked so hard to get better.

"Yeah." He chuckled into the phone. "Michael, my PT, likes to push me, which translated into English means he's a total masochist and exercises the shit out of me. I'm just about dead when I get home."

"But you're improving," I said. "I can see how much better you're walking now and I know your fingers are more flexible because your piano playing has improved a lot." Somehow it was easier to say those things when he wasn't in the room with me.

There was a hiccup of silence, then: "Thanks Ivy. That means a lot coming from you."

My heart skipped a beat. "So— " I tried to sound light and breezy but my heart was racing inside my chest— "what do you need help with in French?"

He went over the areas where he was having trouble— some conjugations and sentence conversions. It only took me about ten minutes to walk him through it.

"How do you know so much about French, Ivy?" Q asked when I'd finished explaining. "Do languages just come easy to you?"

I laughed. "I don't know. I've always been sort of obsessed with France. I love the country, I love the history, I've always wanted to visit Paris." I shrugged, even though he couldn't see me. "So I've studied extra hard to learn to speak French."

"Yeah, I liked Paris. It's a very cool city."

I blinked in surprise. "Wait a minute. You've been there?"

"Yeah. A family trip."

"Oh my God, Q!" I couldn't believe it. His cool factor just went up by about twenty points. "Tell me all about it!"

He laughed again, low and sexy. "Can't do it on the phone, Ivy Ly." He sounded regretful. "There's a price for knowledge, you know. But I will tell you this: I've eaten lunch in the restaurant halfway up the Eiffel Tower and been to the Louvre and seen Jim Morrison's grave…." He sighed. "So many details…."

"Stop it—" I groaned— "you're killing me! What's the price?"

I swear I could see him grinning through the phone.

"Go out to dinner with me."

My mouth dropped open in surprise.

"How about this Saturday?"

I panicked. I couldn't possibly go to dinner with Q— Mira would freak. "I..I can't this Saturday. I've got to practice for a concert and…." Q cut me off.

"It's no problem. We'll do it another time."

"Okay." I searched desperately for a compromise. "Can you just tell me a few things?" I was not good at bargaining. Evidenced by the fact I still hadn't told my parents I wanted to study music. "Like, did you go inside the Louvre?"

"Yep. I saw the two triangles, you know—like from the Da Vinci Code? The top pyramid is huge and made of glass.

It's really cool how it juts down out of the ceiling and is suspended above the smaller bottom pyramid, which is stone."

I sighed with longing. "And did you ride a riverboat on the Seine? And—"

"Gotta pay to play, Ivy. Just a simple dinner and I'll tell you everything you want to know." He laughed. "Listen, I've gotta run. Thanks for the help. *Au revoir*."

Q DIDN'T MENTION Paris the next day and I didn't bring it up either. Though I tried to convince myself otherwise, it felt like I was treading on quicksand. But I was also dying of curiosity. Q walking the streets of Paris. Somehow that wasn't difficult to imagine.

Mira was back in study hall with us and chattered away about the upcoming play which was entitled 'Bah, Humbug!' —a take on Dickens' A Christmas Carol. She was playing the part of the ghost of Christmas Past and was describing her costume in great detail.

Every once in a while Q would look over and smile, teasing me with an 'I've got a secret' look before Mira would ask him a question, forcing his attention back to her.

OUR DAYS FELL into an easy rhythm as Christmas approached. Q, Mira and I spent third period in French and sixth period in study hall together. Q had physical therapy after school every day. The one day we'd gone to the Java Hut his therapist had been out. Mira seemed to be falling harder for him. I'd stopped talking to her as often because I couldn't stand to listen to her go on and on about him. It made my stomach ache and my heart hurt. Which totally sucked, because if there was ever a time I needed a best friend, it was now.

Q was definitely getting better. His handwriting was improving, as was his memory. He was almost caught up in his classes and I knew that he wouldn't need my help much after the Christmas break. Which should have been a huge relief.

I practiced like crazy on my piano for the Christmas concert. I was playing the showcase piece for the youth symphony again, but this would be for an even bigger crowd, so that much more pressure. The piano was the one place where I could lose the voices in my head that tormented me all the time. I don't know what I felt for Q, but if this was love, I didn't want it. Not under these circumstances.

Chapter Thirty

Kellen

There was only one week left of school before the Christmas holidays. I was oddly conflicted about it. Two weeks without homework sounded awesome. Two weeks without Ivy didn't.

I straightened my tie in the mirror. The white silk was a stark contrast to the black shirt and jacket I wore over a pair of dark jeans. I smiled at myself. My lips only had a slight drag down on the right now. Barely noticeable. Almost normal.

My right hand was still messed up, but it was improving. I picked up the football sitting on the nearby dresser with my left hand and held the ball while I stretched the fingers of my right hand around the pebbly leather. I gripped the ball and cocked it over my shoulder, then I turned and threw it at my bed. More spiral than wobble. There was hope.

The chimes of the doorbell rang through the house. I hurried down the stairs in the rambling hop-skip movement I'd developed to favor my right foot but my mom still got to the door before me. I think she'd been sitting there waiting to see who could have possibly coerced me into this deviant behavior. When I'd told her I was going to a youth symphony concert she hadn't believe me at first.

"That's funny, Kellen. If your sister had told me that, I'd believe it, but you—not so much."

My sister, Julie, was a major music geek, which was my way of saying she was a music major. She played the violin and had always been going to this symphony or playing in that concert when she was in middle school and high school. For a kid who loved football and sports it had been excruciatingly painful for me to sit through all the boringness. When she left for college I swore I would never go to another one.

From the middle of the stairs I could see my mom open the door. Her back went rigid as she considered the girl before her. Standing on the porch, illuminated in a pool of light, Mira stood in a one-shoulder black and white zebra-striped dress. Her bright red lips were hardly noticeable because her hair was striped black and white too. Her hands were covered with black silk fingerless gloves, and she twirled a mask that was attached to a stick.

"Ah, h..hello," my mom stuttered.

"Hi," Mira said in a perky voice. "I'm here for Kellen."

"Hi Mira," I called as I hopped the last few steps. I put my arm around my mom's shoulder. "Mom, this is Mira Stouffer, Mira this is my mom, Jane."

Mira put her mask up to her face and peered at us through the oval eye slits. The mask was zebra striped as well, with red rhinestones around the eyes and running down the nose.

I didn't have the heart to tell her that masks were more of a Mardi Gras thing than a symphony concert thing.

"Nice to meet you," she said.

"Right, then." I stifled a chuckle. I was enjoying myself more than I probably should have been. "Gotta go." I kissed my mom on the cheek, ignoring her partially opened mouth. I grabbed the bouquet of red roses that I'd left on the entry table. "I'll be back before midnight."

"Bye." Mira fluttered her fingers at my mom, who still stood gaping, and headed back to her car.

"Mom." I pointed to my chin. "Your mouth." She snapped her mouth closed.

She glanced at Mira's departing back and whispered to me: "Kellen Michael Peterson – don't tell me that's your *girlfriend?*"

I smiled at her. "I'm trying to expand my horizons, Mom." Then I closed the door behind me and followed Mira to Jefferson. I only bumped my head on the window once on the ride to the concert hall.

IVY DIDN'T KNOW I was coming to her concert tonight. Mira had invited me.

"I thought maybe you'd like to see what she does for fun," Mira had quipped. I think she was surprised by how fast I said yes.

"That's a nice touch," Mira said, nodding at the roses. "Who are they for?" I couldn't tell if she was serious or not.

"Uh, well, Ivy— " I tried to hide my embarrassment— did she think I'd gotten them for her? "I figured flowers would be safe." I didn't dare admit how long it had taken me to choose just the exactly right 'safe' thing. I tucked the flowers on the floor under my seat.

I recognized a few kids from school in the crowd, mostly orchestra geeks, as I escorted Mira in to sit down. I tried to ignore the stares as people did double-takes at Mira's outfit. Somehow standing on my porch freaking my mom out had been kind of funny. Being seen as Mira's "date" at this concert was something different. The idea of fleeing before I was seen entered my mind. But I was here for Ivy, not Mira, so I gritted my teeth and pretended I couldn't hear the whispers.

The concert hall was really a beautiful old church, with soaring ceilings and an ornate balcony that wrapped around the room. Mira pointed out people she knew.

"There's Mr. and Mrs. Ly."

I glanced over curiously. I could see Ivy's features in her mother's elegant face. We had seats in the center with a good view of the stage. I pointed toward the cello section. "Is that Brandon Chang?"

Mira leaned close to me. "Oh yes. He and Ivy have played in orchestras together since fourth grade, I think. They've known each other forever." She barely took a breath. "He used to date Jenny McNamara but they broke up right after Homecoming." She nudged my elbow. "I think he saw Ivy in her Cinderella dress that night at the dance and fell in love with her. She was so beautiful." Mira had a dreamy smile on her face. Then she sobered. "That was until you puked on her."

It was like falling off the high dive in slow motion.

"*What?*" I jerked my head to look at Mira.

She put her mask up to her eyes and peered at me through the glittery slits. "Don't you remember?"

I wanted to yank the mask out of her hand and hit her over the head with it. But I just shook my head as a terrible kind of dread filled me. I pointed toward my ear. "Brain injury, remember?"

"Oh, right, that." Mira dropped the mask. "We were all standing around talking to Jazzy and Ollie. You walked up with Laurel Simmons and right when Ivy turned around you ralphed all over the front of her beautiful dress. Then you passed out."

This was a new kind of humiliation. I wanted to sink low in my seat and cover my head. I'd puked all over Ivy at the Homecoming Dance? Why hadn't anyone told me? I'd embarrassed myself before, but total humiliation over something I didn't even remember doing was new.

"Did she at least get to enjoy the dance?" I asked, already knowing the answer. I hadn't been at the dance very long before I'd been taken to the hospital.

"Nope." Mira shook her head with annoying matter-of-factness. "She didn't get to dance or even get her picture taken in front of the Eiffel Tower. And she loves Paris— " she cocked her head at me— "did you know that? She was so excited about that miniature Eiffel Tower. It's her dream to go there one day. Well— " she flopped a hand to the side— "it's both of our dreams but I figure Ivy will be the one to get there. That girl knows what she wants."

The musicians were beginning to warm up, with their see-sawing squeaky sounds as they tuned their instruments. I watched Brandon Chang tune his cello, immaculate and confident in his tux. I imagined what Ivy must have looked like at the dance. So beautiful that Brandon fell in love with her, even though he was with another date. That was, until I puked on her. God—no wonder she didn't like me. But I didn't think she liked Brandon that much either—or she wouldn't have kissed me back that day.

I opened and closed my right hand against the side of my leg, working the muscles, but also to let out some of my nervous energy. I had decided I was going to ask Ivy to break up with Brandon and go out with me.

THE CONCERT STARTED right at the dot of seven-thirty. I enjoyed the music more than I would have expected. I guess all those years of listening to my sister play had developed some appreciation for the symphony against my will. A little more than halfway through, they took an inter-mission. Several of the musicians got up and readjusted the brown folding chairs as others rolled out a black baby grand piano. They positioned it right in the center of the stage and an odd nervousness quirked my heart. It was the same feel-ing I got just before a game.

The conductor took center stage and faced the audience. The crowd quieted down to total silence as he spoke. "And now, it is my special pleasure to introduce an exceptionally gifted student. One who not only excels at the violin but also is, in my humble opinion, a virtuoso pianist. Please welcome Miss Ivy Ly." He swept his arm out.

The crowd was very appreciative as Ivy entered the hall from a side door. She was wearing a black glittery dress that hugged her slim figure in all the right spots. Her long dark hair was pulled back from her face and pinned to the crown of her head, falling in a cascade of curls down her back. An odd kind of pride filled me. To say she looked beautiful seemed inadequate. She was a star.

She didn't look at the audience as she took her place at the piano. I saw her nod at Brandon as she went past. I fig-ured the look on his face wasn't so different than the one on

147

mine. That he got to know and share this side of Ivy and I didn't made my stomach clench.

Mira grabbed my fingers and squeezed. "Here we go," she whispered. She didn't let go, leaving her hand clutching my fingers. I looked down at our entwined hands, feeling claustrophobic. I smiled at her as I freed my hand. Not sure where to put it where she wouldn't grab my fingers again, I stretched my arm out along the back of her seat. That felt better. I ignored it when Mira shifted in her seat so she could lean her head against my arm.

Ivy ran her fingers over the keys and the orchestra immediately sat at attention, their arms cocked above their instruments, waiting. She was the quarterback, making the call to the rest of the team. A new sense of respect filled me.

She didn't have music—she played entirely from memory. Her hands flew in complete mastery of the keyboard. I watched in awe. The pieces she played for me in fifth period didn't begin to touch the complexity of what she played tonight. The orchestra created background tension as the music moved from tender to frenzied to haunted. She played the piano like I'd never heard it played before. It wasn't notes that flooded the room where we sat—it was emotions.

When she finished, the final notes fluttered in the room like a beating heart, until I swear my heart beat with the same rhythm.

She lifted her fingers from the keyboard and an awed silence filled the room. Capped by thunderous applause.

Then she stood up and bowed.

The entire audience jumped to their feet in a standing ovation. I'd never experienced such a rush of pride in someone else's talent before.

I put my fingers to my lips and let out a piercing whistle of appreciation. Her head turned and she looked straight at me. Even from that distance I could see the surprise on her face as she recognized me.

Chapter Thirty-One

Ivy

I was shocked to see Q standing in the audience at the concert. He was hard to miss—all 6' 3 of him, standing up, whistling and clapping like I'd just intercepted the ball or whatever was important in football. Of course Mira brought him, but she hadn't given me a clue that she'd been planning anything.

My mother and father stood nearby as lots of people congratulated me after the performance. But Q's tall figure, hovering on one side of the room, pulled at me like a magnet. Finally, it was their turn. Mira squealed and hugged me.

"Wow, look at you," I said, taking in her zebra-awesomeness. "That's a new outfit."

"I know," she said, holding up her mask and peering at me through the eye-slits. "I've been saving it for this special occasion." Then she turned and looped her arm through Q's like he was her boyfriend. "Look who I brought with me!"

It was like a needle pierced the happy bubble around my heart as it suddenly all became clear. Mira brought Q because she wanted to go on a date with him, nothing more or less. She hadn't brought him to see me. Who knew why he came.

"And we match!" Mira chirped. "He's the male version of a zebra in his black and white." She waved her hand up and down in Q's direction. "You know, the understated version."

I'm not sure Q knew he was dressed like the male version of a zebra. He looked slightly ill at Mira's announcement, which made me smile. But aside from that, he looked very handsome, like normal. I'd never seen him in a tie before. He wore it well—with confidence— like he was used to attending the symphony or something.

"Whatever, Mira," Q said, rolling his eyes. "I'm not gonna touch that." He handed me a bouquet of long-stem red roses I hadn't noticed him holding. His face sobered. He looked very sincere. "You were amazing, Ivy."

"Thank you." I said as I took the flowers, which were long-stemmed and the deepest velvet red. "There are beautiful. And thanks for coming. That was a surprise." I bent to smell the roses and noticed that tucked among the stems were several strands of plumeria. Where had he found plumeria in Washington State in December? Startled, I looked up at him. "More surprises?"

His eyes were intent upon me. "I love plumeria." He said it so softly that at first I thought I'd imagined it. My heart dropped into my stomach before it zinged around like the ball in a pinball machine.

My lips curved. "Me too."

Mira looked from me to Q and back again. "What are you two talking about?"

Just then, Brandon walked up. "You were fantastic, Ivy!" He gave me a hug and let his arm linger possessively around my shoulders as he turned to face Mira and Q. A weird expression flickered across Q's face before I dropped my gaze.

"Aren't you two the cutest couple," Mira said with a giggle and looped her arm possessively through Q's. "We should double-date!"

LATER, I WOULDN'T allow myself to think about Q. When I'd introduced him to my parents at the concert, there was part of me that wanted to cry. I wanted to tell them that finally, I had found the boy that I loved. But of course, I couldn't. Mira was very possessive of him and acted like they'd been together for months. Q hadn't responded to her suggestion that we double-date and I had a feeling that Brandon wasn't terribly interested in that idea, either. I couldn't decide if Q was ignoring how Mira was acting or if he was just oblivious. On the way home, my mom commented on what a nice boy Mira was dating.

I woke up Sunday with a terrible sore throat and a fever. My mom took me to the doctor on Monday. Strep was the verdict. Germs were the culprit. Antibiotics were the cure. But I knew perfectly well it was totally emotional overload. I sent Q a text saying that I was going to be out sick for a few days. He asked if I needed anything but I said no. I don't think he would have understood if I told him I needed a surgical excision of my heart.

IT WAS A GOOD thing to have distance from Q. I was tormented by my feelings for him and then tormented over the guilt over my feelings, then tormented by my lack of feelings for Brandon until I was afraid all my tormented feelings would choke me. Mira Skyped with me every day, bless her, but she talked about Kellen non-stop. I finally told her I couldn't talk about him anymore or I would barf. Which was pretty much the truth.

I DIDN'T RETURN to school until Friday, the last day before Christmas break. My mom wanted me to stay home one more day, as we were planning to leave the next day for the holidays, but I told her I needed to check my assignments—even though I'd been getting them online all week. She'd trained me well to be responsible. I really went back to school because I wanted to say goodbye to Q. My family was going to be traveling to New York for the holidays to see my brother, as well as to visit my aunt and uncle. I wouldn't see Q until after the first of the year.

FRIDAY FLEW BY. Q asked me in first period what I was doing over break. I told him we were traveling almost the entire holiday and after that he hadn't talked much. I'd asked him if he was traveling but he said no, his family was taking a big trip during spring break.

It seemed like I blinked and we were in fifth period. Like normal, Q and I were alone in the music practice room, sequestered in our own little world. We hadn't talked about my concert. We hadn't talked about Mira. We hadn't talked about anything. We were like two strangers, paddling through a dark current, together, alone. If that made any sense at all. Waiting to see if we were going to survive the rapids or die plunging over the falls.

Q sat down at the piano, but he only played for a few minutes before he stopped. His fingers were still resting on the ivory keys when he turned toward me.

"Ivy, I've been wanting to ask you something for awhile." My heart skipped a beat. "What is it?"

"If you could have your pick of any college—where do you want to go?"

I'd never actually given an honest answer to that question before—not even to my parents. I always cloaked the truth in several options. I guess I didn't want to say it out loud for fear I wasn't accepted and then would have to admit my failure. But now, for some reason, I told the truth.

"I'd like to go to Harvard. That way I could make both my parents and myself happy. That would be my first choice."

He nodded. "They'd be lucky to have you." He slid sideways and straddled the bench facing me. "Would you study music?"

I blinked. No one ever asked me that question. Everyone just assumed that I would study medicine. But the truth was, I had other plans. "I've never really told anyone this before, but yes, I'd like to."

The surprising thing was, he didn't look surprised at all.

"Have you always known what you wanted to do?" Q's words were hushed.

I nodded. "I've known for a long time. My parents started me on the violin and piano at age three. They are very—" I hesitated, searching for the right word— "*focused.* I excelled at both instruments so they became more focused. But I think their intent was simply to develop my brain so I would be better prepared to pursue medicine as a career."

"They want you to be a doctor?"

I nodded. "I never had the heart, or the nerve— " I shook my head at my own lameness— "I don't know what—but I never told them I had a different dream."

Q was quiet for a moment. "My sister knew from the fifth grade what she wanted to do, too."

"What about you?" I ventured. "Have you always known?"

"Me?" He leaned his head back to gaze at the ceiling. When he looked back at me, his words were hushed. "I always loved to play football, but mostly because I was so good at it. I was always tall for my age and athletic—it just came easily to me. Then over time, everybody just expected me to keep playing." One side of his mouth lifted in a smile that was more mocking then genuine. "After awhile I forgot there were other choices." He fanned his hands in front of himself. "They told me I was going to be a star." His expression sobered. "I'd never once considered that the choice might be taken away from me. And certainly not now—right when my dream of playing Pac-12 ball was just about to come true."

I could see the raw wound in his expression, hear it in his voice. The emotions he tried to hide all the time were painfully obvious.

"That's why I work so hard at getting better," he said softly. "I'm not sure what else I'm good enough to do."

There was something so brutally honest about him—so fragile—I dropped my guard and put my hand over his. "But Q, there are always other choices."

All the swagger and self-confidence that used to emanate from him when he strutted down the hallways were gone.

"Yeah, but can we choose them, Ivy?" We sat frozen, searching each other's eyes – recognizing our own reflection in the other. He ran his fingertips along the side of my face, so soft and gentle. "Will we?"

A longing filled me until I wasn't even sure what we were talking about anymore.

"Will you do me a favor, Ivy?"

At that moment I would do just about anything for him.

"Do you remember when I asked you to play your favorite song?" His hand dropped and he threaded his fingers through mine. I felt like I was melting from the inside out.

I nodded. Of course I remembered. I had shocked myself by really playing the song that meant the most to me.

"Will you play it again today?" I couldn't define the conflicting emotions I saw in his face—I was too chicken to ask. "Play it for you and me?"

My breath caught in my throat. They were simple words that didn't convey a simple meaning. *For you and me.* It said something and nothing at the same time. Without admitting anything, it said everything.

"Yes," I whispered.

We switched places and his hand trailed along my back before he sat down in the chair. I put my hands on the keys and looked once at his face, his beautiful face that I had memorized long ago, then I closed my eyes and played from my heart. All the sadness and confusion, the guilt and longing poured out through my fingers. I cried through the music. I held the last note, letting it ring and ache, like my heart did.

I opened my eyes and looked over at him. The silence between us stretched, like a tenuous thread that connected our hearts.

His hair fell across his forehead and shadowed his eyes. On the outside, he looked like a Cali surfer boy, all beautiful and sexy. But the pain in his eyes told me that inside was a different story.

"I look at you, Ivy," he said softly, "and you can do so much. You have so much talent, you're so smart…"

"Stop it." I scooted to the edge of the piano bench. My fingers brushed his warm skin as I swept his hair out of his eyes. I cupped the sides of his face with my hands—the growth along his jaw rough against my fingers. My heart ached with the love I had for this man-boy.

"Q, you are a star," I whispered. "You're so smart, such a hard worker. Everyone loves you." I spoke slowly. "You are meant to do great things. You inspire others to do great things." I smoothed his hair again, loving the feel of it against my fingers, the chance to just touch him. "You *will* do great things. I know it. Just follow your heart. The rest will fall into place." And then I kissed him. With all my heart.

He kissed me back, so tender and sweet. His hand crept up and entwined in my hair and he pulled me closer. His lips parted mine and our tongues met. I could taste him, tangy-sweet like cherry coke, and smell the fresh scent of soap on his skin. I loved every thing about him.

"Ivy." He pulled back, his voice soft, his fingers still wrapped in my hair. "We have to talk."

I sat back. Dread replacing desire. Don't make me say it. Plead ignorance. "About what?" For just this one moment I'd given into my feelings. No one would ever know.

"About us." He pushed himself out of the chair and slid onto the bench beside me. His blue eyes bored straight into my soul. "We can't keep pretending there's nothing happening here."

"Q." My voice sounded small, which is how I felt. "There can't be an 'us'." My heart broke with every word.

His brows pulled down in a frown. "Why not?"

My eyes pleaded for understanding. "Because my best friend has been crazy about you for over a year. It would break her heart if you and I went out." A single tear slipped from the corner of my eye. "I could never do that to her."

"Are you talking about Mira?" He sounded shocked.

I nodded. "Remember what she told you that first day in study hall?"

"You can't be serious." He honestly didn't seem to know that Mira thought she loved him. "Who says something like that and actually *means* it?"

"Mira." I ran my hand along his cheek, looking up into his blue eyes. I needed to soak it all up in this moment because I knew we would never be here again.

"Ivy, I like Mira but I wouldn't date her in a million years." He sounded desperate. "I think about you all the time—I wonder what you're doing, if you'd like certain things. I *miss* you when you're not here. I've never felt like this about anybody before." He cupped my face in his large hands. "I want to be with *you*, Ivy, not Mira." Then he kissed me again—slow and sweet and wonderful.

"Hey guys!" Mira's voice called from around the corner. "Are you ready to go to study hall?"

We jerked apart just as her stunned voice said, 'What the *hell* is going on here?"

Chapter Thirty-Two

Kellen

Ivy jerked away like somebody had stabbed her. Our heads swiveled toward Mira at the exact same moment. I'll never forget the look on Mira's face right then: her mouth hanging open in shock. A pair of felt reindeer antlers were perched on her head and they bobbed with little jingly bells. But in that split-second it was like everything was frozen in time, even the bells. Then Mira turned and ran. Before I could even open my mouth, Ivy jumped off the piano bench and ran after her.

"Ivy—wait!" I called after her.

"I can't! I've got to explain this to Mira." Then she disappeared out the door. I swung around on the piano bench and stared at the black and white keys. How did Ivy think she could undo the truth?

IVY WAS GONE. She had told me they were flying out first thing Saturday morning. It felt like part of me had gone with her. There was so much left unsaid between us.

When Ivy ran after Mira but they'd both apparently left school because I couldn't find either one of them again before classes ended.

I called Ivy later but she didn't pick up. I sent her three text messages. Finally on the last one she responded. I looked at it again on my phone for about the millionth time: *Q I'm sorry. I let things go too far. I can't do this right now. I'll talk to you when I get back.*

My emotions, which I'd thought were finally beginning to level out after my accident, were suddenly back on a roller coaster. And to top it all off, Laurel came up to me at the end of study hall and suggested we get together during break. Talk about timing. She hadn't talked to me in three months and she had to pick today, of all days, to break the ice?

What a shitty way to start vacation.

THREE DAYS LATER Ollie and I were stretched out in the recliners at his house playing Halo 3. For the first time in a long time I was kicking his butt. His parents were at work and it was just the two of us down in the basement. The shades were drawn like usual and the room was mostly dark.

"How's Jazzy?" I ventured, not sure if he wanted to talk about it or not.

"I guess she's okay. We haven't talked much lately." Ollie sounded glum.

"Do your parents know?"

"Not yet." He jerked his joystick up as he tried to make his vehicle jump a gap in the grid but he didn't make it and exploded in a ball of flames. He dropped his hands in his lap with a dejected sigh. "They're gonna fuckin' *freak*." He flopped his head back against the cushion. "God, I can't even think about it. It makes me want to throw up."

I paused the game. I felt depressed for him. Or maybe I felt depressed for me. Or maybe I felt depressed for both of us. Shit - when did life get so messed up? I wanted the rewind button – to go back to the day of the Homecoming Dance and start over. "What's Jazzy want to do?"

He rolled his head over to look at me. "You have to ask?"

I ran my hand through my hair and let my head flop back against the cushion too. "Damn."

"I know. And I love Jazzy. I do. It's just—*God.*"

We sat in silence for a few minutes.

"How's it goin' with the tutor?"

I let out a deep sigh. "Rocky."

"Yeah. Hasn't she got a boyfriend?"

I wondered how Ollie possibly knew that. "Yeah. And there's some other shit goin' on too."

Ollie started the game again. "Forget her, man. Chicks aren't worth it. Get yourself well and go play ball at U-Dub. You'll have it made. With your looks—you'll be able to get any girl you want."

I THOUGHT ABOUT Ollie's advice as I laid in bed that night staring into the darkness. The problem was, I didn't want any girl—I wanted Ivy.

MY RIGHT FOOT and leg had improved enough that my parents finally agreed to let me drive again. It was a thrill to get back behind the wheel of my F150 truck and regain some independence.

I worked out harder than ever during Christmas break. Not only at the gym, but at the piano as well. Coach had asked me to come in and talk about making some updated training films after break that we could send out to the scouts who had offered.

There were some days I was so freakin' tired I wasn't sure I could climb the stairs to my room. But there was no doubt things were improving.

WE CELEBRATED CHRISTMAS at our house. My older sister, Julie, was home from college and my mom's sister and her family always came to celebrate with us. My cousins were close in age to Julie and I. We'd grown up together, though they'd gone to Bellevue, but I didn't hold that against them. Besides, we'd beaten Bellevue this year.

We were all sitting around the dinner table, stuffing ourselves, when Ronnie, my cousin who was a year old than me, asked me how I was doing.

"Pretty good," I said. "I can actually hold a football in my right hand again." I usually tried to answer questions about my health quickly and get on to other topics. I didn't want to talk about all the things I couldn't do now.

"You're not thinking of playing football again, are you?" he asked.

I paused with a bite halfway to my mouth and looked at him in surprise. "Of course I am."

"Dude," he gave me an incredulous look, "you're damn lucky you weren't a permanent stroke victim. Why would you take the chance of messin' yourself up again? Do you have any idea how long it'll take your brain to totally heal from the damage it's already suffered?"

I saw my mom and dad exchange a look. An odd silence settled over the table. I slowly lowered my fork to the plate, suddenly pissed.

"No, Ronnie. I don't know. How long?"

"Years, man. If ever. Your brain probably had to completely rewire that section. Don't you remember they had to drill a hole in your head to take the pressure off so your skull didn't explode— "

My aunt cut him off. "Ron, that's enough."

"What?" He looked over at his mother. "I'm trying to save Kellen from ending up being a vegetable..."

"Enough." The warning glare my aunt gave him should have made his hair sizzle.

I glanced over at my sister, who was sitting next to Ronnie, but she dropped her eyes. Something twisted in my stomach. What the hell was going on?

"It's okay, Aunt Sheila," I said, scooping up a big bite of mashed potatoes. "Thanks for the warning, Ron." I wondered how Ivy's Christmas dinner was going.

Chapter Thirty-Three

Ivy

Of course Mira had to walk in on me and Q kissing. She'd never *once* come to the music room before study hall before—*ever*. But that day, that minute—she had to show up. I ran after her, through the hallways packed with kids, trying to ignore the stares.

"Mira, stop." I pleaded as we reached the parking lot. "Can't we just talk?" Mira just slammed her way out to Jefferson and then jerked the car out of the parking lot. God, why couldn't she drive?

She sent me a text about fifteen minutes later. *'Ur a slut.'*

I couldn't think of an answer to that.

I went back in, got my stuff out of my locker and sent Brandon a text breaking up with him.

What a total loser I'd become.

I walked home and cried the whole way.

WE HAD TO leave at three a.m. to make our six o'clock departing flight. I didn't sleep for one second that night. Everything that had happened—with Mira, with Q, with Brandon— just circled around my head relentlessly like horrible vultures wanting to pick at the remains of my brain. Or maybe it was my soul. It was actually a relief to get up in the darkness and take a shower to get ready to go. At least I had tasks I could focus on rather than the intangible demons of guilt and longing.

CHRISTMAS IN NEW YORK can actually be very beautiful. My aunt and uncle lived in a spacious condo not far from Columbia University that overlooked Central Park.

"See Ivy." My mother nudged me as we sat in their elegant living room with lofted ceilings and expensive antique furniture. "Being a doctor has its privileges along with its responsibilities."

"Yes, Ma."

IT BEGAN TO snow the day before Christmas. I love snow. There is something so magical about it. Within a few hours the city was covered in a sparkling white blanket. It continued to snow over night, grinding traffic to a snarled mess. At mid-day on Christmas, my brother and I put our scarves and mittens on and walked through Central Park.

We followed the path along the lake, beautiful white flakes drifting down from the sky filling the air around us, like magical feathers. The world was soft and beautiful— full of endless possibilities. Well, not endless. Some things weren't possible.

Tuan's hands were shoved into his pockets, his shoulders hunched against the cool air. He had black hair like mine and was lean, taller than my father. Maybe living in America your entire life did that to you, made you taller somehow. He was also very intelligent, working on his medical degree with the intent of being an oncologist, which was a reflection of his kind, sensitive personality. We'd always had a special friendship.

We'd only been walking for a few minutes when he spoke. "What's up, Ivy?"

I didn't look at him. It felt like there was an elephant sitting on my chest, crushing me. I didn't know if I could admit the truth to him without being trampled under the weight of my own emotions.

"Is it the pressure of school?" He reached out and pushed my shoulder. "There's obviously something wrong, little sister. You look like you just lost your best friend."

Of course, then the whole story came pouring out. I told him everything. Every last little bit, from Brandon to Mira, right down to Q kissing me—which I had hardly even allowed myself to think about—and how Q told me he wanted to go out with me. Even as I told my brother a thrill of wonder shot through me at the idea. Why would Q want to go out with *me*?

Tuan was quiet for a long time as we walked, but for the first time in days I felt a sense of peace. It had helped to tell someone else, to let it all out. Finally.

When Tuan spoke, his words were gentle. "It sounds like a tough time, Ivy. I'm sorry you've had to go through it alone. You know you can call me anytime, right?" He tilted his head so he could look at me. His breath came out in puffs of white. "I may be on the other side of the country but we have phones here too."

I laughed and wiped my eyes. When did I start crying? "It just got so messed up so fast," I sighed. "I thought I had

166

it under control. I thought I could stop my feelings for him. I never dreamed it could become so tangled."

Tuan nodded and kicked a snowball that someone had left on the pathway. It exploded in a puff of white. Overhead the trees stretched their arms over us like a protective umbrella, covered in white icing.

"Is he worth it, Ivy?" Tuan's words were quiet, thoughtful. "You'll be done with high school in a few months. Then you'll be off to college where this Kellen fellow won't be attending." He stopped and looked at me, his face etched with pain – for me. "Wouldn't it be better to just stop tutoring him and let him live his life and you live yours? You two come from different worlds: He's a football player – you'll be on to medical school. You have no common interests. What's the probability that you'd date beyond the summer anyway?"

His face became more animated as he talked. Tuan was passionate about his studies. He always had been. But he was the eldest son. That position came with an inescapable expectation in an Asian family.

"It's just by freak chance that you got to know him at all, right?" Tuan started walking and I fell in alongside him, the world suddenly feeling heavy again. "Let your friend Mira have him and you return your focus to your studies and music." He glanced sideways at me. "You're so talented, Ivy. The future can be anything you choose to make it."

My heart felt like it was breaking all over again. Of course he was right. Stop the insanity and get my focus back. Just as I'd always done. Excel, excel, excel – make your family proud, Ivy.

I nodded and pressed my lips together to stop them from wobbling. Against my will, I pictured Q's face as he'd stared into mine, telling me he wanted me. I wondered what he was doing for Christmas.

Chapter Thirty-Four

Kellen

I waited until the day after Christmas to ask my mom WTF. It was obvious that the family had been talking about me behind my back. There were so many things in my life to be pissed off about right now that I didn't even know where to start.

"So Jane," I asked my mom, "what'd you think of Ronnie's comment at dinner yesterday?" I was sitting at the kitchen bar eating a turkey sandwich for lunch. I'd been waiting for the right time to bring it up, but there was never a right time and I couldn't wait any longer.

She jerked her head up from the mail that she was sorting to look at me. I never called my mom Jane. "What do you mean?"

"You know exactly what I mean, Mom. About not playing football." I sounded pissed. I *felt* pissed. "I got the distinct impression last night that everyone else in the room had an opinion on the subject that they hadn't bothered to share with me." I took another bite of sandwich, chewing slowly, trying to remain calm. "Now I want to know what you think."

She dropped the envelopes to the counter. "Kellen, we don't need to discuss this right now. You're just finally starting to feel good again. Let's focus on the positive steps you're making."

I set my sandwich down, an unfamiliar dread twisting my stomach. "No, Mom. I think we do need to talk about it right now." I looked straight at her. "Are you saying that you don't think I should play football again?" My voice echoed with disbelief.

She sighed. "Honey, it's practically a miracle that you've recovered like you have." She sounded like she was pleading.

"Doofus, why would you even consider it?" Julie walked into the kitchen right then. She punched me in the shoulder as she walked by. "God, Kell. Don't be so stupid."

"Julie." My mom gave my sister a look. "I don't think you're helping right now."

"Mom!" My sister wheeled around. "Somebody's got to tell him. It'd be crazy to— "

"Wait a minute." I pushed myself off the stool and stood up. I towered over both of them but suddenly I felt like I was twelve years old again. I had the most terrible urge to cry. "You can't be serious." I looked from one to the other. "After all the years of work I've put into footba— "

"Kellen." My mom interrupted me. She held her hands out. "Calm down. We don't have to make any decisions today. There's lots of time— "

"There's NOT lots of time," I cried, slamming my hand down on the counter. "National Signing Day is the first Wednesday in February. That's barely a month away. You *know* that. Why do you think I've been working so hard? So I can show those colleges who've offered that I'm FINE."

"Kellen, bleeding brains and paralyzed limbs are not *fine*," my sister snapped.

"Shut up, Julie," I shouted.

"You shut up." She yelled at me like only a sister can. "What is *wrong* with you? You don't need football, Kellen—"

"Stop it, both of you." My mom was definitely pleading now. "Let's wait until your father gets home and—"

"Yes I do!" I shouted at Julie. "What else would I do?"

I was surprised at the surprise on her face. Her mouth dropped open and honest-to-God, for a minute it was like she couldn't get any words out of her mouth. That would've been a first. But of course, she recovered.

"Jesus Christ, Kellen. Are you *serious*?"

"Julie—" now my mom snapped— "watch your language."

"You can do anything." Now Julie was shouting. "I've worked my ass off all my life to make the grade. *Everything* comes easy to you. You're smart, you're athletic, you're good-looking, you have lots of friends." She flung her hands out. "Has there ever been *anything* you've ever wanted that you didn't get?"

Ivy, I thought.

"Both of you." Now my mom was shouting. "Stop it, this instant."

"I've worked for everything I've gotten," I said, glaring at my sister.

"Well, then work at staying *alive*, you dumbshit." Julie slammed a cupboard door. For a second she looked like she was going to cry. "I know." Her eyes narrowed and her tone changed to pure sarcasm. "You used to want to be a doctor. Why don't you work on being an orthopaedic surgeon so you can save all the *stupid* football players who aren't as lucky as you and have to spend the rest of their lives in a wheelchair using a feeding tube?" She stormed out of the kitchen before I could think of a reply. What the—

I swung around to face my mom.

"Take a walk, Kellen." Her tone was non-negotiable. Coach Branson had nothin' on my mother. "We can talk more when you've calmed down." Then she left the room too.

THE LAST TIME I cried was when Laurel broke up with me. Which wasn't that long ago. I hoped this wasn't becoming a pattern. I walked for a long time. Darkness comes early in Washington in December. Today, I was glad. I could hide in the darkness.

Somehow I ended up at the high school football field. I climbed the steps in the stadium up to the very top and stared down at the dark field. There were a lot of good memories associated with this place. They rolled through my head like a Powerpoint display.

I wanted to talk to Ivy so bad I ached. Somehow I knew she could make sense of my confusion. Ivy, better than anyone, understood the pressure I felt to succeed. I tried to imagine the sound of her voice, but instead, the image of her tipped over in the back of Mira's orange VW giggling her head off interrupted my thoughts.

I tried to remember what she'd said to me in the music room, the last time I'd seen her. Right before she'd kissed me. But the memory of her lips against mine and the sweet smell of plumeria filled my head instead. I wondered if things had improved between her and Mira.

I pulled out my phone and punched in her number. The telephone pad on the screen of my iphone glowed green with her numbers highlighted at the top. Would she pick up if I called? I wanted to talk to her so badly. My heart gave a nervous thump in my chest. Only one way to find out. I jabbed the 'call' button and put the phone to my ear. I slid my other hand into my pocket, and stamped my feet to get warm, my breath puffing out in a frosty cloud.

"Please pick up, Ivy," I whispered. "*Please.*"

Chapter Thirty-Five

Ivy

I stared at the phone as it buzzed in my hand. There was one letter in the contact name area: Q. My fingers tightened on the edges. He was so close. It was like I could touch him through the phone. My heart pounded. How I wanted to hear his voice. To ask him what was happening between us?

But I sent the call to voicemail and turned my phone off.

I was awake for a long time thinking about what Tuan had said.

Chapter Thirty-Six

Kellen

On New Year's Eve Ollie and CJ picked me up and insisted that I had to go to a party that Jake Bellarmine was having. I really wasn't in the mood, but I wasn't in the mood to stay home either.

There'd been no further discussion of me playing college football. By the time I came home that night of the fight I was too exhausted to think about it anymore and had just gone to my room. Ivy never responded to my call.

"DO YOU GUYS ever think about what you'd do if you didn't play ball?" I asked. We were in Ollie's truck headed for the party. They were passing shots from a Cuervo bottle 'hidden' inside a brown paper bag. Like that'd fool the cops if we got pulled over.

"Not play ball?" CJ glanced at me with a confused look. "Why in the *hell,* would we ever think about that?" He nudged Olli's arm. "Life is all about playing ball, if you get my meaning."

Ollie laughed and raised the brown bag. "Amen, brother."

I felt like saying 'and look where that got you,' but I didn't. I leaned forward so I could see both of them at once. "No, I'm serious. Are you loading all your bets up on that one thing and just letting it ride?" I thumped back against the seat, and rested my elbow on the window frame. "What if you get cut? What if you get injured? Don't you think you should have a plan B?"

I wasn't sure why I was asking because I knew both Ollie and CJ didn't have a plan B. They'd been all about football forever. Just like me.

"We just got to make it to the big dance, baby, and we've got it made," CJ said. "The good life is waitin' for us."

Ollie could tell something was buggin' me. He leaned over his steering wheel to see me. "Why you asking, Kell?"

I hesitated for just a second, almost afraid to say it out loud. But I pushed the words out of my mouth. "Because there's part of me that thinks maybe the Homecoming game was my last dance."

JAKE LIVED IN a big house not far from Springwood. The party was rockin' by the time we got there. Apparently Jake's parents were in Seattle for a wedding reception and were spending the night there. When we drove up the drive-way was full and cars lined both sides of the street. It looked like every light in the house was on.

"Don't park too close," I warned. "This place is just beggin' to get busted."

Ollie parked about a block away on a side street. That way if we had to run for it, we could disappear through the yard and get away without his truck being seen. CJ tucked the brown bag in his back pocket as we walked up to the front porch.

From outside, the music wasn't too loud, but when they opened the front door, it poured out in a wave of sound. CJ was in the lead, then Ollie, then me. Even as I walked in the door, I wasn't sure I wanted to be there.

I leaned forward and yelled in Ollie's ear, "Where's Jazzy?"

"She's at home. They've got family there all week. Plus—you know." He kind of shrugged. "She'd be pissed if she knew I was here."

"Kellen! Ollie! Over here."

I raised my hand at a couple of teammates who greeted me from the far side of the room. "When are you going to tell your parents?"

Ollie shrugged. "Soon. I don't want to talk about it right now, okay?"

"Sure. I don't blame you." And I didn't. What a thing to have hanging over your head.

IT WAS FUN to be out with my friends, after all. After my accident it seemed like I'd lost my old life in the blink of an eye. Ever since then, I'd been hiding, trying to get better, trying to catch up in my studies—trying to figure out how to find myself again.

Suddenly, here I was.

I'd grown up with a lot of these kids since grade school and everybody seemed glad to see me. A number of the girls gave me the impression they'd be more than friends if

176

I was interested. I was chatting with Caroline Bennett and Hailey Swenson when somebody came up from behind and wrapped their arms around my waist. A soft chest pressed into my back.

"Hi Kellen," a sexy voice whispered in my ear.

Caroline rolled her eyes with an annoyed expression and Hailey looked at the person behind me then at me, as if waiting for a reaction. There was no question whose voice it was: Laurel's.

I disentangled her arms from around my waist and took a step away before I turned to face her.

"Hey Laurel." Mr. Super-Casual. No letting on how much it'd hurt when she'd dumped me last fall. I held a red plastic cup in my left hand and slid my other hand—my bad hand—into the pocket of my Levi's.

"You look good, Kellen." She traced her finger down my chest, her hips too close to mine.

She looked good. Her pale blond hair was down tonight and she wore a tight black V-neck sweater that prominently displayed her ample cleavage. Her jeans were low and tight and part of her flat stomach peeked out when she raised her cup to drink. Even in December she was tan. All over, from the looks of it. A few memories flashed before my eyes— half-dressed memories—and I took another step back.

"I didn't know you two were still friends," Hailey said to me.

"Me either." Caroline looked angry as she took a drink. "Where's *Josh*, Laurel?" she snapped. I wondered what was up with that. Caroline and Laurel used to be best friends.

"Didn't you hear?" Laurel tilted her head up to look at me as she answered Caroline's question. I could tell she was drunk. "Josh and I broke up. He's a free agent now." She wavered on her feet as she gave me a seductive smile. "And so am I." She staggered a step back and looked down her nose at Caroline. "Why don't you go check him out—you might have a chance now."

"No thanks, Laurel," Caroline sneered. "He's more your type than mine." She barely gave me a glance. "See you later, Kellen," she said as she walked away. I sensed she'd just insulted both Laurel and Josh but I hadn't exactly followed the thread. Girl fights were strange and dangerous things and usually never about what was actually being said.

After Caroline departed, Hailey didn't stay long. She mumbled something about finding more beer and wandered off, leaving Laurel and I semi-alone. I took a drink and looked across the room. Ollie and CJ were standing together in an opposite corner, both watching me. CJ gave me a thumbs up and grinned as he did a little hip thrust, but Ollie dropped his gaze to Laurel then looked back at me and raised his eyebrows.

I shook my head. Been there, done that. Not going back again.

"I've mistyou, Kellen," Laurel said, sliding her words together. "You look s'good. Are you all well?" She threaded a finger through my belt loop and tried to pull my hips toward hers. "Y'know—well enough?"

For a half a second I was tempted. She was damn good-looking. But she wasn't the same Laurel I'd started dating a year ago. She'd changed and God knows I'd changed. As CJ had called it at the game, somewhere along the line she'd become a definite skank. Maybe she always had been and I'd never looked past her beauty. I thought of Ivy and what a completely different class of person she was. Thank God I'd elevated my standards.

178

I smiled. "I'm doing great, Laurel. Thanks for asking—finally." It took a moment for my sarcasm to sink in. Her face shifted from the sexy tease to guilty surprise with a side of too much innocence.

"What do you mean?"

"It doesn't matter anymore. I'll see you around, Laurel." As I walked away I heard her whimper behind me.

"But Kellen—wait—"

But I didn't wait. And I didn't look back. It felt good to close the door on that one. Ollie wanted to leave around 11:30 so he could call Jazzy at midnight. By then, I was ready to go too. I still fatigued easier than I used to, and I really wasn't into drinking anymore. My head was messed up enough as it was.

CJ said he'd catch a ride with a couple of the other guys, so Ollie and I took off.

"Did you tell Laurel to piss off?" Ollie asked as he pulled away from the curb.

I laughed. "Hopefully with a little more class than that, but basically yeah."

"Good." He sounded pleased. "After what she did to you, she deserves it."

I sensed more behind his comment than the obvious. "What do you mean?"

He looked over at me in surprise, like he realized he'd said more than he should. Then he shrugged. "I guess it doesn't matter now, but she was bangin' Josh behind your back while you were in the hospital."

Even though I didn't care, something twisted in my stomach and made me feel slightly sick. I guess betrayal is always bad, whether you think you care or not.

"But the best part of that —" Ollie continued, "is that Josh has been cheating with Cindy Morris behind Laurel's

179

back and just dumped Laurel." Ollie laughed out loud. "What goes around, comes around, brother."

Suddenly Caroline's comments were starting to make more sense. I laughed. "Just keep her away from me."

Ollie's phone buzzed. He pulled it out of his coat pocket while he held the steering wheel with one knee and started texting a reply.

We swerved sharply to the left and crossed the centerline.

"Ollie!" I barked at him.

He caught the wheel and jerked back into the other lane, over-correcting. Gravel spun out from the right side of the road as we swerved back into our lane.

"Holy shit!" I cried, gripping my arm rest and the dashboard. I sure as hell didn't need to get in a car wreck.

"Sorry man. Usually I can do that and text just fine," he laughed. "I guess I had more of that Cuervo than I realized."

"Just don't do it while you're driving." I sounded pissed, but he'd scared me.

"Yeah, yeah." He grinned at me and slid his phone back in his pocket. "Guess what?"

"What?" I was watching the road, suddenly wondering how messed up Ollie was.

"I'm going to ask Jazzy to marry me."

I jerked my head over to stare at him. "What?"

"Hey, I'm gonna have a kid. He needs to grow up in a proper family. I love her an' I'm gonna do right by her."

"Well, that's awesome, Ollie." I slapped him on the shoulder. "Congratulations. Jazzy couldn't ask for a better guy."

"Yeah, I know." He grinned as he pulled into my driveway. "Good luck with the tutor, bro. Why don't you send her a midnight text? They love that romantic shit."

I TOOK OLLIE'S advice and texted Ivy right at the stroke of twelve. I didn't expect a reply but I was glad that she knew I was missing her. I was so ready for her to come home.

AT TWO O'CLOCK my phone buzzed me awake. I squinted at the green numbers on my clock. Man, who was calling me at this hour? I grabbed my cell and looked at the screen. A picture of Laurel from last summer, bent forward to reveal her cleavage while she blew me a kiss, stared back at me. What the hell did she want?

I stared at the picture for another second before I sent the call to voicemail and set my phone back on the nightstand. I rolled over and pulled a pillow over my head. I didn't even want to know what she wanted. One minute later my phone started ringing again. I snatched it up: Laurel again. Still blowing me kisses.

I groaned and punched the answer button. "What?" I sounded groggy.

"Kellen, I need shoo." She was so drunk I could barely understand her. "The cops came an' bushted the party an' it wash crazy. We ran an'— " she burped in my ear.

"Whoa, slow down, Laurel. First off, where are you?"

"I'm right outshide your window."

"What?!" I jumped to my feet and ran to the window. I jerked the curtains aside and looked down in the yard. The light from the streetlamp illuminated enough of our yard to see through the murky shadows. Sure enough, Laurel was lying flat on her back on the grass looking up at my window. She waved when she saw me.

"Jesus Christ," I muttered as I pulled a pair of jeans on. It had to be in the 40's outside and she didn't even have a coat on. "Don't move," I barked into the phone.

"Okay Shellen." She giggled drunkenly into the phone. "I mean Kellen."

I debated whether to wake my parents as I hop-skipped down the stairs. It was two in the morning – better not. I was just shoving my feet into a pair of boots when my mom called from upstairs.

"Kellen, is that you?"

"Yeah, it's me, Mom." Now was one of those times when honesty was the best policy. "Laurel's outside drunk. I'm going to take her home." I yanked my ski coat on.

There was a moment of silence. "Do you need help?"

"No, I got it covered, Mom. Go back to bed. I'll be back in a few."

"Be careful."

I RAN THROUGH THE GARAGE and out through the side door. I kept my truck parked outside so at least I could pour Laurel directly into it without having to try and navigate the garage. I could see her still lying in the same place on the grass. I ran up. "Laurel, get up. I'll take you home."

"Shelley." She had one eye closed and her teeth were chattering. "Everything is spinning. I feel sick."

I rolled my head back and exhaled a cloud of white as I stared at the sky. Why me? I bent down and slid an arm under Laurel's shoulders. She was ice-cold. "Sit up." I propped her into a sitting position intending to take my coat off, but as soon as I let go of her she flopped back down like she was Gumby or something.

I yanked my coat off and wrapped it around her, then hefted her up into my arms and hurried to my truck. Thank God my right arm was so much better. I braced one leg on

182

the tire and supported Laurel on my lap as I dug the keys out of my pocket. She wrapped her arms around my neck. "I…I l…love you, Kellen." Her teeth were still chattering. "I..I alwaysh h…have. I just din't know what to do when you were hurt."

"Yeah, whatever."

I flipped the unlock button and managed to pull the door open and heave her inside. I didn't even bother with the seat-belt. She was so wasted, if we crashed, I was pretty sure she'd just bounce anyway.

I ran around to the other side, hopped in and gunned the engine. We hadn't even got to the end of the street before Laurel puked in my truck.

I'LL NEVER FORGET the look on Mr. Simmons face when he opened the door at 2:30 in the morning and I was standing there supporting his shit-faced daughter. Even though I wasn't guilty of anything but trying to help, my heart was racing like a sprint car as he opened the door.

"Good evening, sir." I was talking fast—trying to explain before he made the wrong assumption. "Laurel showed up at my house a few minutes ago and needed a ride. She doesn't seem to be feeling well." I looked down at the obviously drunk girl slumped in my arms. "And I loaned her my coat." Jesus. "I'm just trying to help her, sir," I added hurriedly.

A string of unintelligible words poured out of Laurel's mouth as she peered up at her father. Her lipstick was smeared, her hair was a mess, beneath my coat her clothes were askew and she smelled like vomit. I didn't even want to think about what the inside of my truck smelled like.

About a million expressions went across Mr. Simmons face in the ten seconds it took him to assess the situation. Then he put his arm around his daughter and helped her into the house. "Thank you, Kellen." It was all he said before he shut the door in my face.

I stared at the closed door, thinking about how odd life was. "Happy New Year, sir."

Chapter Thirty-Seven

Ivy

I GOT A TEXT from Brandon a couple of days after Christmas.

Hi Ivy. How's the Big Apple? I heard there's a ton of snow. Hope you're having fun. I don't want you to feel bad about breaking up. We're better as friends anyway. See you when you get back. BC.

I cried when I read his message. I never used to cry. Now I cry about everything. What is wrong with me? It was just that he knew me so well. It seems like we should have been a perfect couple, but it was more like he was my other brother. I always knew we were *too* much alike. Maybe Brandon liked someone else too. I hoped so. At least he didn't hate me. I was pathetically grateful.

I hadn't heard anything from Mira, but I hadn't contacted her either. I figured it would be better if I just waited until I got home. So she could call me names to my face. I wasn't even going to let myself think about Q.

MY FAMILY STAYED up and celebrated New Years Eve at midnight. We blew horns and laughed and danced and watched the ball drop on TV. It was a bittersweet moment. I would rather have been with Mira and Q, but I was glad to turn the page and start a new year too. This year I was going to be in control of my life. And my emotions. And stay focused.

Chapter Thirty-Eight

Kellen

On New Year's Day I drove out to Bayside Park, which is a hilly, wooded park that runs alongside—wait for it—the bay. I parked in the lower parking lot and got out and walked. The paths were well groomed, with lots of big hills that wound through old-growth forest. Not surprising, the place was practically deserted in the frosty January weather.

There was no particular destination that I had in mind. I just needed to get some air, to be alone – to have some time to think. To try and figure out what was going on between me and Ivy, between Ivy and Mira, and if I was honest, to try and figure out if I was really and truly done with Laurel forever.

She'd called me earlier in the day to apologize and to thank me for bringing her home. Sick, hung-over and busted by her parents, all the obnoxious bullshit she put up trying to be cool and popular had been deflated. On the phone, she'd sounded like the shy, quiet girl I used to know.

"Hi Kell." It was like a voice from the past.

"Hey. How're you feeling?" I could just imagine. Her picture had come up when she called so I knew it was her, but still, there was a bit of a nervous twinge in my stomach when I'd answered.

"Mortified," she whispered. "I don't even remember how I got to your house. Or the ride home."

"Don't worry about it, Laurel." I slid my hand into the pocket of my jeans and walked to my window. I stared out at the cool, grey day, the brown, bare tree branches a stark reminder that we were in the heart of winter. "I'm just glad you got here. You were freezing when I put you in the truck."

"You probably saved my life." There was a long silence. "Not like I deserved it."

"Don't say that, Laurel." And I meant it. "We all make mistakes."

"My biggest mistake was when I lost you, Kellen." Her words came out in a rush. "Do you think we could start over? Go back to the beginning and try again?" I closed my eyes. I could picture her back then—so sweet and pretty. So different than she was now. She sounded like she was crying. "I really do love you."

My grip tightened on my phone. "Laurel— " What was I supposed to say to that? "Let's just give it some time, okay?"

"But you're not going out with anyone, are you?" She sounded desperate.

I couldn't be going out with Ivy if she was still going out with Brandon Chang, could I? "No, but—"

"Just think about it." I couldn't help but hear the hope in her voice. "You won't regret it Kellen. I promise."

188

IT WAS A good workout climbing up and down those hills. But I could handle it. My leg had built up enough strength again that I didn't become fatigued anywhere like I used to. But my head was going in circles. Ivy wouldn't go out with me because Mira liked me, but my gut told me that Ivy liked me too, even though she was going out with Brandon Chang. Now Laurel wanted to get back together. Which I have to admit, a month or two ago I probably would have jumped at the chance. Even talking to her today brought back memories and they weren't all bad.

I'D BEEN WALKING for almost an hour when I stopped at the top of a hill and braced my hand against the rough bark of a giant Douglas fir tree. I was at the edge of a cliff that dropped straightaway to the rocky beach below. Puget Sound stretched before me, the grey-blue waters constantly in motion with little waves as the tide rolled in. The cries of seagulls split the air as they wheeled and dove above the water. The sharp salty scent of the sea was fresh in the air and I breathed deeply.

My family had hiked often when we were growing up and I loved the outdoors. It gave me a sense of power, surrounded by the majesty of nature. Like anything was possible.

The conversation I'd had with my mom after my first day of school suddenly came back to me. Her voice was clear in my head. *'If you make up your mind to play a sport—you will. If you make up your mind, Kellen—anything is possible. You just might have to go about it a little differently than you originally planned.'*

I watched a seagull drop a shell on a rock and then swoop down and grab it, only to fly up and drop it again. After five tries, the shell had cracked enough that he could eat the insides. It reminded me of Coach Branson's talk to us during the last dance, which was how I thought of the Homecoming game now. *'Because the difference, gentlemen, between winning and being a winner is in never giving up. Try again, give it your best every time—and I guarantee you— you'll all be winners.'*

The seagull suddenly flew up the cliff and perched on a limb above me. I swear the thing looked straight at me, his head cocked to one side, and let out a piercing series of cries. Out above the water, another seagull answered him. And just like that—I knew what I had to do.

YOU SAID IF I ever needed somebody to talk to I could call you. Can you meet me?

I re-read the text one more time before I clicked send.

AN HOUR LATER I was sitting waiting for Mira at Pioneer Park, a big complex of outdoor soccer fields that were unused this time of year. I saw her little orange VW coming down the hill toward the park so I got out of my truck and leaned against the side of it, waiting for her. She pulled up and turned the engine off. I could see cautious curiosity in her face as she waved at me through the window.

I opened her door for her and leaned down. "Want to sit in my truck? There's a little more room."

"Sure." She grabbed her shoulder bag and slid out of the car.

I stared at her in amazement. "Mira, what are you wearing?"

She glanced down. "Oh, yeah." She shrugged. "I don't know."

It was the first time I'd ever seen Mira dressed normal. She had on a pair of gray converse sneakers, a pair of skinny leg blue jeans and a black jacket. She was completely non-descript. Even her hair was one color. I almost asked her if she felt all right, but then I wasn't sure if that would be insulting or not.

I opened my door for her and gave her a hand up into the cab, then jogged around the back of the truck and climbed in. I had the engine running as it was getting colder by the minute. They were predicting snow any day.

She turned and sat at an angle in the seat, close to the door. "So what's up?"

"I need your help, Mira."

She blinked in surprise. "You do?"

"Yes." I nodded. "There's been a terrible misunderstanding that needs to get straightened out— "

"Oh." She leaned back and crossed her arms. "That."

"I need your help and advice, Mira."

Her lips twisted. She cocked her head and gave me a sideways look. "This is about Ivy, isn't it?"

"It's about you—" I spoke slowly— "and me—" I kept my words soft— "and Ivy." I put my arm along the back of the seat until I could almost touch her. "I think it's important that you know the truth."

"About what?" Her voice was dry. "Best friends who lie?"

"No." I kept my voice steady but firm. "About best friends who blame the other because they're not getting their way."

Her eyes narrowed. "What do you mean?"

I kept my voice low. "Mira, you're not mad at Ivy because she likes me. You're mad at Ivy because I love her."

Mira sucked her breath in and her eyes got wide. I wasn't sure if she was more shocked at my accusation or at the

191

fact that I had admitted I loved Ivy. Which actually sort of shocked me, too. But now that I'd said it, I knew it was the truth.

"That's not true." Mira cried.

"I do love her, Mira and I'm going to fight for her. But the truth is, *I* was the one who kissed Ivy that day in the music room when you walked in. She had just finished telling me that she would never date me because *you* liked me. She chose you over me. But you wouldn't listen to her—you wouldn't believe her—so I'm here to set the record straight."

Mira turned away from me but I saw the tear that ran down her cheek.

"You and I both know that we're never going to date. Under any circumstances." I paused to let that sink in. "Don't we, Mira? We're better as friends."

Mira sniffed and stared out the window again, her fingers clutched tight to her crossed arms. Even her fingernails were plain, like she'd somehow erased herself. There was a long silence before I spoke again.

"I'd like for the three of us to be friends, like we used to be. That's why I called you, Mira. I need *your* help to fix the mess that I created between the two of you."

Mira's chin wobbled and she turned away to look out the side window. "What do you want me to do?"

"Could you stop being mad at Ivy for something she didn't do? Could you just talk to her?" I leaned over and put a finger under Mira's chin to turn her head so she had to look at me. "She's been as good a friend to you as anyone could ever ask for. Don't you think you should return the favor?"

Chapter Thirty-Nine

Ivy

WHEN I WOKE UP on New Year's Day shafts of sunlight were streaming through the white curtains of my room, like rays of hope. I was snuggled in bed with my big fluffy white comforter and fuzzy socks on my feet. I'd had a dream where I was laughing with Q and Mira, sitting on a blanket in a big field. It had been summer. The happy remnants of my dream still clung to my memory and I felt oddly content.

Out of habit, I reached for my phone, though I'd received no messages since Brandon's three days before. I'd never been a big texter. Except to Mira. To my surprise, there were two text messages. I quickly slid the access bar on my phone that opened my text message folder.

Happy New Year, Ivy. I miss you.

When are you coming home?

They were both from Q. The first message had come in at 3:00 am exactly. That would have been 12:00 am in Seattle.

Midnight on New Year's Eve. Instead of being with some-one else, he was thinking of me at the stroke of midnight. I felt like he'd sent me a New Year's kiss.

I hugged the phone to my chest as a thrill of joy shot through me, followed quickly by a pang of sorrow. I missed him, too—desperately. And Mira. Before I could talk myself out of it I quickly typed a reply: *Tomorrow.* And hit send. Nobody could twist that into something it wasn't. I was just being polite. I kissed my phone, right where his message was.

FOUR HOURS LATER I got a text from Lily. *Mira went to The Crypt with Tank & got totally wasted. Tank was play-ing in the band & Mira spilled some guy's drink & he started a fight and Charlie Jackson had to defend her. It was really bad. What's going on with you two? When are you coming home?*

I wasn't going to tell Lily what the real trouble was between me and Mira. *We're leaving tomorrow. Is Mira okay?*

Yes but she's really being weird. I've hardly seen her all break. Hurry up. We need you.

WE WENT HOME the day before school started. I was so ready for this break to be over. There were things I needed to fix.

Chapter Forty

Kellen

On Monday, the first day back, I got to school twenty minutes early, just to see Ivy. I stood in the hall outside our Calculus class waiting, feeling pretty much like an idiot. Finally, at quarter to eight I went into the classroom. I was the first one there. That was a first in more ways than one. Mrs. Cooper gave me a surprised look.

"Do you have a question, Mr. Peterson?" Her lips pressed together in an old lady pucker.

"No, M'am. Just early for class."

She peered at me over her glasses, waiting for the catch.

"A New Year's resolution?" she said drily.

Really, I didn't know the old bird had a sense of humor. "Something like that." Luckily, other kids started filing in through the door then. I opened my book, but I kept looking at the door. Where *was* she?

Jesse Martin, one of our defensive backs, sat down on the other side of me. "Hey Peterson, did you have a good break?"

I turned to talk to him. "Yeah." Which was a total lie. "You?"

I smelled Ivy before I saw her. God, I loved the smell of plumeria. I jerked around and there she was. Her hair swung forward, shielding half her face as she sat down, slightly out of breath. She was wearing a red sweater the color of holly berries that made her skin look so rich and brown, her hair all black and shiny.

I'd had all these things I was going to say. All these ways to be cool and impress her and instead I just smiled at her. "Hi Ivy." I felt such a sense of peace. She was home.

She looked a tiny bit flustered when she looked over at me, but she smiled like she meant it. "Hi Q." Her eyes kind of lingered on mine for a little longer than normal. She had the most beautiful eyes I'd ever seen.

"All right, students." Mrs. Cooper stood up. "I hope you all looked at your math assignment over break…." A groan went up in the class.

"Welcome home," I whispered.

LIKE NORMAL, Mr. Pruitt was in a nasty mood in second period science. We couldn't even talk.

"Have you talked to Mira?" We were on our way to third period French, the class we shared with Mira. Girls were so different than guys. I figured I better be prepared if there was going to be a cat fight. Ivy was walking next to me and that protective urge came over me again. I just wanted to put my arm around her shoulders and protect her. To let everybody know she was mine. Which, of course, was about a million miles from the truth.

"Nope. Radio silence." She looked up at me. "I think it will be better if Mira and I can talk one on one."

"Yeah, well, let me know if you need me to run interference." Her brows twisted at me in a confused look. "Football term. You know—let me know if you need my help."

She half-laughed. "Oh. Okay."

MIRA WAS SITTING on the far side of the room from where we usually sat when we walked into the French room. She appeared to be completely dressed in black, like she was headed to a Goth party. Or a funeral.

"Apparently still pissed," I said under my breath.

"Apparently."

I glanced at Ivy in surprise. I hadn't actually meant for her to hear that. But she seemed fine. She sat down and got out her notebook and stared toward the front of the class at the teacher.

I sat at an angle in my chair, partly to give my legs room to stretch out, partly to be able to watch Ivy. I could see Mira look our way several times, but she never met my eyes. I'd told her what I thought. I was going to leave it to the two of them to figure out the next step.

IVY AND I split up for lunch and fourth period. I liked sitting with the guys at lunch. It was the same crew I'd hung out with basically since sixth grade. We had two or three tables we filled up every day and I figured Ivy was probably happy to get away from me for awhile.

Today, though, for the first time, I contemplated leaving the guys and sitting with Ivy. I knew she wouldn't want to sit with my gang. I searched the lunchroom for her but I couldn't see her anywhere. I looked for Mira but I couldn't find her either.

I HURRIED TO fifth period. Michael had me running now and had started using some weights with my right leg. I didn't even limp when I walked anymore and only had weakness when I was really tired. For the first time since the accident I believed that I was going to get well. I'd been practicing with CJ and actually had been passing right on the money. It was a good feeling. Coach had more workouts planned for me, too. If I survived, I was going to be in better shape than I'd ever been in my life.

I hurried into the music room. I couldn't wait to show Ivy how much I'd improved on the piano. I had a surprise for her today, partly to repay her for how much hard work she was doing for me.

I dropped my backpack on the floor and pulled out my piano book, fanning the pages to find the piece I'd secretly been working on. It was a piece by Brahms, set in a minor key, so it was haunting and beautiful. It totally reminded me of Ivy.

Spreading the pages out on the stand, I started warming my fingers up, a strange little bubble of nerves in my stomach, like I was warming up before a game. I heard Ivy talking to someone in the choir room behind me so I stopped playing. I wanted the music to be a surprise. Instead, I started playing some other warm-up scales as I waited for her.

After a few minutes I glanced over my shoulder. I could see her standing in the doorway as she finished up her conversation. It looked like she was talking to one of the music teachers. Her long dark hair fell down her back like a wall of black silk, and even from here, she looked exotic and beautiful. That sense of pride I always felt when I was around her filled my chest. Did Brandon Chang have any idea how lucky he was?

Ivy hurried in my direction. "Sorry I'm late. Mr. Flynn needed to talk to me about something." She only carried a notebook to fifth period rather than a backpack as she didn't need any books. She dropped gracefully down into the folding chair, sliding her feet beneath her. She motioned to the piano. "You can go ahead and start. You don't need to wait for me."

I opened my music again and adjusted the pages, suddenly feeling nervous and sort of lame. But I plunged ahead. "I worked on a new piece over Christmas break."

"Oh, that's great." She gave me a teasing smile as she leaned back in the chair. "So you actually practiced?"

"Yeah." I laughed. "A little." If she only knew. I'd started learning this song during Thanksgiving break. It had taken me this long and too many hours of practice to count, to play it well enough for her to hear.

I was going to give her some bullshit line and pretend to be super-cool to hide my embarrassment then I changed my mind. I just told her the truth. "This song is my thank you for all the help you've given me. I think of it as Ivy's Song."

"What?' she said softly. She got a look just like my mom does when she's going to get all emotional. Just like that, the nervous bubble was gone. That expression on her face was worth every hour of practice I'd put into this song.

I placed my hands on the keys and exhaled. My fingers found the first familiar notes and from there it just got easier. I only fumbled one little part but the rest of it went pretty damn good. I played the last arpeggiated chord and glanced over at her.

Her eyes were all watery like she might cry. "Oh my God, Q, that was wonderful. I can't believe how well you played! Honestly, you're amazing." Suddenly she had her arms around my neck and her voice was soft in my ear. I could feel her wet cheek against mine. "Thank you. I couldn't have asked for a more precious gift."

I didn't think—I just reacted. I slid my arms around her back and pulled her close, burying my face in her soft hair. She fit just right against my chest. For one freaky moment I thought *I* might cry. I took a deep breath of plumeria. I'd done it.

For the first time since my accident I was proud of something I'd accomplished. Something besides regaining what I'd had and lost. I'd done something new. Score one for the TBI boy. Just then Brandon Chang called her name from the orchestra chamber room.

"Ivy, Ivy—did you hear?"

She jerked out of my arms as Brandon came rushing through the door. I silently groaned and clenched my fist, wishing I could pop the little orchestra geek in the nose. Clearly, we needed to start shutting the door to this room.

"We've been accepted! We're going to Paris over spring break!"

Chapter Forty-One

Ivy

Brandon slid to a stop as he spotted me and Q, even though I'd hurriedly slid back into my seat.

"Oh," he said. It was like there was a tickertape running across his forehead as he put two and two together. "Uh. Sorry." Brandon's face went blank and he pushed his black frame glasses up his nose. Then his excitement bubbled over again. *But did you know?*"

I nodded. "Mr. Flynn told me when I got to fifth period." Out of the corner of my eye, I saw Q's head swing toward me. He had the strangest expression on his face.

Suddenly he pushed the piano bench back with a terrible screech of the wooden legs against the linoleum tile floor and stood up. "Sounds like you guys have some exciting plans." He grabbed his backpack and swung it over his shoulder, his muscles bulging through his sleeve. "I'll let you get to it. I've gotta check in with Coach Branson about something anyway."

For a second I was so surprised I didn't say anything. "But Q, wait—"

"See you later." He headed for the door without a backward glance.

Brandon gave me a silent, wide-eyed look as he stiffly raised his hand toward Q. "Kbye." He kind of looked frightened. Which was a little bit funny in a not-funny-at-all situation.

I jumped out of my chair and ran to Q's side, grabbing his arm. "Do you have to go now?" He had a look I'd never seen on his face before. Angry and disgusted and—*wounded*.

"Yeah, Ivy. I do." Then he jerked the door open and walked through, not giving me any room to follow him.

Q DIDN'T COME to study hall sixth period. Of course, Mira wasn't there either. I waited twenty minutes before I packed my stuff up and walked home. I wanted to text Q. I wanted to call him. But one part of my head kept whispering: This is the break you need to tell him.

I thought about the beautiful song he'd played for me. Ivy's Song. It made me smile just thinking about it. I'd never been given anything more precious and heartfelt. But his gift also made me want to cry at the same time, making my decision that much more painful.

Chapter Forty-Two

Kellen

I couldn't get out of school fast enough. Thank God I had a doctor appointment for an excuse, though I would've left anyway. I couldn't go sit with Ivy in sixth period knowing that she and Brandon were going to Paris together. An orchestra trip together was one thing, but *Paris?* Seriously?

I'd been so excited to see Ivy, to play her song—to show her how much I'd improved— I'd forgotten the little detail that she was still going out with Brandon. But dammit, if she liked Brandon so much, why did she hug me and look at me like that?

I kicked an empty soda can that was lying near the garbage can. The tinny clang echoed off the school's wall as I strode out to the back parking lot. Shit! Why did this have to be so difficult all the time? Why did I have to care?

EVEN THOUGH I drove to my doctor appointment, my mom insisted on coming too. Julie had left on New Year's Day and gone back to college. We never did talk about 'the fight' again, but it hung in the air around us like the dog's fart. You couldn't see it, but everybody knew it was there.

My mom sat next to me thumbing through a magazine as I was texting a couple of the guys while we waited for the doctor. The endless piano practice had definitely improved my right hand. My fingers actually responded like normal to my brain now, which made me grateful every time I used them.

"Ron is studying to be an occupational therapist," she said out of the blue.

I didn't stop texting. So. We were going to talk about it. "That's nice." I clicked send and shoved my phone into my pocket. "Is that what makes him such a know-it-all?"

"Kellen." That disapproving tone. "I think he spoke out of true concern for you, not to be a know-it-all." My mother closed the magazine. She was really pretty cool. She rarely freaked out about anything. "I think we should ask the doctor what she thinks about you playing football again."

DOC MURDOCH WENT through all the standard tests and questions before she took my right hand and tested my fingers. When she set my hand down and looked me square in the eye over her glasses, my heart gave an extra beat. Something was coming.

"You are truly amazing, Kellen. It's practically a medical miracle that you could recover like you have. Especially in that amount of time." She put a hand on my shoulder. "It's a testament to your hard work and the power of believing in yourself."

"Thanks, Doc." I wondered what she would think if she knew how many times I hadn't believed in myself. I shrugged. "I'm feelin' pretty good again."

"How's your school work going? Do you still need a tutor?" She peered at me with a look that said she already knew the answer.

The truth was I didn't *need* a tutor. But I *wanted* my tutor. In more ways than one. "Nah, probably not. I'm caught up in everything now."

She nodded and turned away. "I'd say that you have officially recovered, Kellen. I don't need to see you again unless you feel like you're having trouble with something." She scratched some notes into my thick file.

"Doctor Murdoch, we do have one question." My mom sat in the blue plastic chair on the other side of the small room, her legs crossed and hands resting in her lap. She looked perfectly relaxed as if this question didn't hold the answer to my entire future—my entire life.

"What's that, Jane?" The doctor turned and peered over her glasses at my mom.

"What do you think about Kellen playing football again?" The words hung in the air. My heart was beating like the drum roll the band played at kickoff.

The doctor glanced over at me as she thought about the question. "From a medical perspective, Kellen's brain and body have had time to heal and are responding normally again. Technically he's cleared to play football."

My heart fluttered in my chest like it had grown wings.

"However—" the doc's tone held a note that made my heart plunge into my shoes— "it's my personal and professional opinion that he would be putting himself at a catastrophic risk to play sports where he might continue to absorb high-level impact to the brain."

She tapped her finger on my file and totally reminded me of Coach Branson. "There's new research from Purdue University that suggests all football players, even those who haven't suffered a concussion or serious injury like Kellen, are receiving sub-concussive blows to the head that are resulting in long-lasting brain impairment. These repeated impacts are causing significant systematic changes in their brain functioning."

Dr. Murdoch crossed her arms. "New studies are showing increased levels of tau proteins in the brain. This occurs when the brain is shaken too hard and the nerve fibers are torn, releasing the tau. The end result is a condition called chronic traumatic encephalopathy, or CTE. There is a conclusive link between tau and brain damage."

She closed her file with a snap and cradled it in one arm. "We're just now beginning to measure and track the damage that the brain and neural system incurs from repeated impact. The long-term effects remain to be seen, though dementia and mental illness seem likely."

Dr. Murdoch slid her glasses down even further so she could see straight into my eyes. The final stab to my heart—I could see it coming. "I've known you since you were an infant, Kellen. I've watched you grow into a wonderful, kind and responsible young man, so I say this not only as a doctor, but as someone who cares about you."

For one heartbeat, the room was absolutely silent. Then came the kill shot. "If you were my son, I'd strongly advise you against ever playing football again. It'd be no different than playing Russian roulette with your brain."

Chapter Forty-Three

Ivy

I went in and spoke to Mr. Decker before school the next day. Before I changed my mind.

"Yes, Miss Ly?" The principal sat behind his big desk, stacks of paper surrounding him, looking pre-occupied. "How can I help you?"

"I think I have to withdraw from tutoring Kellen Peterson." I tried to sound professional. "He seems to be doing much better and I'm afraid that I won't be able to keep up with my own studies and music over the next few months if I keep doing both."

"Hmmmm," Mr. Decker said. "Have you discussed this with Kellen?"

I nodded. "Kind of." Liar! my head shouted at me.

"You sound a bit indecisive, but if Kellen feels that he's recovered enough to resume his regular schedule then it's fine with me." He sat forward and wrote a note on a piece of paper. "I'll let his parents know."

My stomach sank into my shoes. I hadn't thought about Kellen's parents. Would they be upset?

Mr. Decker peered at me across the desk. "Thank you for all your hard work, Ivy. You've been very gracious with your time and I know it was a tough load for you to carry. But Kellen is an exceptional young man and I wanted to make sure he got back on his feet. I'll be writing you a letter of recommendation and making the appropriate notations on your transcript."

I stood up, suddenly sick to my stomach. I'd done it. "Thank you Mr. Decker."

MY FEET DRAGGED all the way to first period. Now I *had* to tell Q. My mother's no-nonsense voice echoed in my head. *"You must face life's difficulties with your head held high, Ivy, and forge ahead."* I thought about what my mother and father had overcome to live in America. To give me and Tuan a better life. I should be counting my blessings instead of being such a cry-baby. I'd be out of high school in less than six months. Time to grow up.

Q WAS ALREADY in class, facing the front of the room when I got there. No part of that was normal. At least the seat next to him was vacant. I marched up and whispered in his ear before I lost my nerve. "I need to talk to you after class." He barely looked at me.

"Okay." He didn't say *whatever* but it was implied as clearly as if he'd shouted it at me. I sat down and felt like I was shrinking, like Alice in Wonderland. What had I done to make everyone I cared about hate me?

AS SOON AS we were out of the classroom I blurted it out. "I'mnotgoingtobeabletotutoryouanymore." I said the words so fast even I couldn't understand myself. My hands were shaking.

He frowned at me. "What?"

"I'm not going to be able to tutor you anymore." I couldn't look at him. "It's too much with all my other studies plus—" I finally got up the nerve to glance at his face—"you don't need me now."

Q stopped in the middle of the hall and turned to face me. Kids streamed around us like fish swimming upstream in a river of bodies. One hand held his backpack strap over his shoulder and the other was shoved into his pocket. He was like some beautiful modern-day version of *the David*— except with clothes. But his presence was every bit as powerful. I clutched my books to my chest, feeling small and insignificant.

His lips pressed together in a bitter line and for a fleeting moment I thought he was trying not to cry. Then his eyes narrowed and he sneered at me.

"Ivy, you don't have any idea what I *need*."

He seemed so far away at that moment—so untouchable—it was like we were back at the start of school again and I'd only seen him from afar through Mira's obsessed eyes. I didn't know him at all. I don't know why I ever thought he might care about somebody like me.

His eyes were cold as he glared at me. "At least you could've been honest about the real reason. But thanks for your help." Then he turned and walked away.

Now I knew what it meant when somebody says a part of them died. A part of my heart died right in that second.

Chapter Forty-Four

Kellen

I went straight to the counselor's office and changed my schedule. There was no way I was going to practice piano with Ivy or sit in study hall and pretend everything was okay.

It wasn't.

Nothing was okay.

Not football. Not school. Not my brain. Not my heart. Not my life.

I headed out to the parking lot to ditch school. *Everything* that I wanted was out of reach. I'd never felt so lost in my life.

"Kellen!"

I ignored the voice and kept walking.

"Wait up." I could hear the clatter of boots behind me as Laurel ran to catch up. "Hi," she said breathlessly as she pulled up alongside me. Her blond hair was blown back and her chest was heaving from her little run, making it hard to look away. "Where are you going?"

"I'm leaving." I forced my eyes away and kept walking.

"For the day?"

"Yep."

She tugged on my arm. "Where are you going?"

I stopped and turned to look at her. "I don't know. Just out of here."

She still sounded breathless but her eyes were shining. "Can I come?"

Chapter Forty-Five

Ivy

Q must have left school, because he wasn't in any of his classes the rest of the day and he didn't show up for piano.

Those terrible words he'd sneered at me echoed in my head: *at least you could've been honest about the real reason.* What did he think the real reason was? I didn't know for sure, but I had a sick feeling he thought it was because of Brandon. I'd never told him that we'd broken up.

Q had left his sheet music sitting on the piano when he'd walked out the day before. I'd tucked the pages into my bag, intending to give them to him today. Instead, I pulled the music out and sat down at the piano. I could see where he'd lined through the title and written *Ivy's Song* in block handwriting. A pang went through me.

I played the piece slowly, savoring the bittersweet melody that seemed to pierce my heart. Every note of the song was like a secret message from Q. When it was over I closed my eyes and played other songs from memory, sorting out my feelings through the black and white keys.

When I'd made up my mind in New York to stop tutoring Q—to fix the problem between me and Mira at any cost—I never dreamed it would be this painful. I'd been so consumed about not upsetting Mira that I'd forgotten to consider that Q might be in need, too. He'd not only lost significant motor skills, but he'd lost the ability to play football, the game he loved and had planned his future around. And he'd lost his girlfriend. All in the same moment.

At a time when he probably needed somebody the most—I'd walked away.

My heart broke and shattered into a thousand pieces, but I knew there was no other way.

WE WERE EATING dinner when my phone buzzed in my pocket indicating an incoming text. Then it buzzed again. My mother didn't allow cell phone use at the table. I swear, curiosity will be the death of me one day. I slowly pulled my phone out of my back pocket. No fast moves around my mother. I even took a bite of food as a diversionary tactic as I juggled the phone around to my lap. I dropped my eyes to see who was texting me.

"Ivy, put your phone away. You know the rules." I don't think my mom even looked at me. That woman could keep me under surveillance from the corners of her eyes.

"I just want to see who it is." I risked it and took a quick peek. Dang! The screen just read TEXT MESSAGES (2). That didn't tell me anything I didn't already know. I slid the bar across my phone and punched the text message button. What a rebel I'd become.

"Ivy Thi Ly." My mother was looking directly at me. "What is so important that you have to interrupt dinner?"

"Binh." My father spoke to her in Vietnamese. "Let it go." My father didn't stand up to my mother very often, but when he did, everyone paid attention. To my surprise, he leaned over and patted my arm. "You're a good girl, Ivy." Then he went back to eating.

My mom and I looked at each other in surprise. Then my mother looked away first. I couldn't believe it. We'd just had a seismic shift in the Ly household, but unbelievably, I was more curious about who was texting, which was a different kind of seismic shift. God, what was happening to the world?

I glanced down to read the texts. My heart skipped a beat when I saw the first one was from Mira: *Can we talk?* Followed by a second message: *I've got Twinkies.*

AFTER DINNER I replied: *Sure. When?*

MIRA PICKED ME up in Jefferson an hour later. If my mom knew Mira and I were having a fight, she didn't let on.

"It's a school night, Ivy. Is your math done?"

"Yes, Ma. And I practiced my piano at school." I didn't tell her *what* I'd practiced, however. "Plus, I've already done violin." I leaned down and kissed her cheek. "I won't be too late."

"Is Mira still dating that nice boy we met at your concert?"

I turned back in surprise. There had to be something strange in the water. Or maybe—and this thought scared me a bit—my mother knew a lot more about my life than I gave her credit for. Sneaky, that woman.

214

"No, Ma. She never dated him. They're just friends."

"Ummm hmmm." My mother was knitting a sweater for Tuan. She didn't look up from her flying knitting needles. "Don't be late."

"I gotta go, Ma. Love you." I ran for the door. I couldn't possibly decipher the coded messages my mother might be sending me right now. I was already on emotional overload.

I ran down the porch steps toward Jefferson, excited and nervous, too. It was so weird— everything was just exactly the same as always, but it was all so different, too. I was going to let Mira do the talking first. Hopefully, she wouldn't yell at me. Or call me names. Inside my mittens I crossed my fingers. On both hands.

I opened the door and peered into the car. "Hey."

Mira looked over at me and smiled. Even though she'd re-done her makeup I could tell she'd been crying. "Hey."

I gasped. "Mira, what are you wearing?"

Mira looked down at her outfit as if she couldn't remember. Regular skinny leg blue jeans, a plain black hoodie— even her hair was all one color: sort of a blondy-brown. I'd never seen her look so bland before. I hated to admit it, but she was dressed like me.

"Oh yeah. Q said the same thing the other day."

I stiffened at the mention of Q.

She waved her hand, motioning for me to get in the car. "Are you going to get in? It's freezing out there."

I slid into the seat and slammed the door shut. Mira shifted into gear and glided backwards out of my driveway.

"Wow." I looked at her in surprise, forgetting I was going to let her talk first. "That was smooth."

She braked to a stop and pushed the clutch in as she ground the gears into first. "I know," she grimaced. "It only

215

seems to happen in reverse though." Then she let the clutch out and we jerked down the road.

It was dark, but not as dark as normal because we had a snow sky. When it snowed around here, it was like there was a big light on above the clouds, that illuminated everything, so you could see perfectly well, even though it was normally pitch black at nine o'clock at night.

I sat with my hands on my lap, my fingers crossed inside my red mittens, and waited for Mira to start talking. I had no idea where we were at in the fight. She had to give me a sign.

She turned the corner and shifted into third as we motored past the high school. The stadium, which was used as a community sports field, was lit up for a soccer game. I could see people huddled in the stands.

She took a deep breath. "Q asked me to apologize to you."

I froze. This was not what I'd expected. "He did?"

"He told me that you told him that you wouldn't date him because I liked him and that I was being a selfish pig for being mad at you for no reason."

I frowned as I tried to decipher what she'd just said. "Q said that?"

"Well—not exactly. But that's what he meant." We sailed past the dark windows of the South Street mini mart where kids went to buy candy and pop during lunch, even though Griffin was a closed campus. "And he was right."

I unclenched my fingers a little bit. Not all the way – but a little.

"I was wrong, Ivy and I'm sorry." She stared straight ahead as she drove. "I shouldn't have acted like that. I shouldn't have said those things. Q's never been interested in me. Not even for a minute. It's always been you." We turned and drove past the graveyard. I could see all the grave markers stretching across the field in the milky light. "I guess I've always known it, too—I just didn't want to admit it." She peeked a glance at me. "Can you ever forgive me?"

I was silent. I wasn't sure what to make of all her ramblings about Q. Since when did she have a window into his soul? Based on this afternoon, not only did Q not have any interest in me, I don't think he even liked me. I pulled at the end of my mittens. "Will you take back the slut remark?"

"Oh yeah, that." She gave me a guilty look. "That was pretty bad, wasn't it?"

"Yeah." I looked out the window. It still hurt to think about it.

Mira gripped the steering wheel with both hands and stared straight ahead. "You know I didn't really mean it. I was distressed."

"As Ron would say, you were completely mental."

"Harry said that."

"Whatever."

"Sorry."

"Okay."

Mira jerked her head toward me, her face lit up with hope. "You forgive me?"

"Yeah."

"Oh, get the Twinkies out of the back seat! It's time to celebrate." She stared talking fast, suddenly sounding like the old Mira. "I've been sick to my stomach the whole entire break." She downshifted to make a turn and we jerked around the corner. "I didn't have anything to do, and I didn't have anyone to talk to and there was this terrible night with Tank and CJ was there and he had to save me—" she groaned— "it was like I didn't even know who I *was* anymore." She waved at her jeans. "And look at how I'm dressed!"

I uncrossed my fingers and reached for the screamer strap. "Yeah, I missed you too."

At that moment snowflakes drifted down out of the sky and landed on the windshield.

Chapter Forty-Six

Kellen

First period Calculus was weird without Ivy there but Jesse sat by me again. He kept a running dialogue of cracks about Mrs. Cooper that sort of made me laugh. When I wasn't thinking about Ivy. Which was never.

Science was science—enough said. I walked into French and scanned the room for Mira. She was sitting on the far side again, doodling in her notebook. I walked over and sat next to her. She wore a green fitted jacket over a short checked skirt. Purple striped socks stretched over her knees and her hair was pink. I took her bizarre outfit as a good sign.

"Hey Mira. You look..um..nice."

She looked up and smiled. "Hey Q." She pointed. "Your leg must be feeling better, you don't even limp anymore."

I nodded. "I'm gettin' there."

She went back to doodling in her notebook. "I talked to Ivy last night."

I tried not to show my interest. "How'd that go?"

Mira looked over at me and smiled. I noticed for the first time that her eyes were green. I wondered if that was her real color or not. They were pretty. "Good. We're friends again."

"Good." I nodded at her, a small bubble of hope rose in my chest. "And Mira—thanks."

She smiled. "You're welcome."

CJ FLAGGED ME down after third period. "Hey Peterson, I heard Laurel showed up at your house on New Year's Eve."

I don't know why I was surprised he knew. There were no secrets in this school. I wondered how long it would take to get out that Laurel and I had ditched school together yesterday.

He peered closer at me. "Are you guys going out again?"

"No." I kept moving down the hall. "Were you lookin' for me?"

"Oh, yeah— " he jerked a thumb over his shoulder— "Coach wants to see you."

"Okay. Thanks. Catch you later, man." I was headed to the gym for fourth period so I made a detour to Coach's office. As I knocked on the blue metal doorframe I wondered if Laurel would tell people about yesterday. My stomach twisted. Nothing had happened. We'd just driven down to the beach and spent the day there. It was over a two hour drive to the ocean and I'd gone there partly so no one would see us together. What would Ivy think if she knew?

I pushed the thought away. Why did I care? She was going out with Brandon. I leaned my head in the door. "CJ said you wanted to see me?"

Coach looked up from where he was working on a diagram of something. His flattop was the same year round, as were his white and blue Griffin Eagles t-shirt and dark blue gym shorts over bowed legs.

"Oh, Kellen. Yes, yes, come in." He set his clipboard aside and shuffled through some papers. "I'm glad Charlie found you. I've got some….." he paused as he dug through another stack of papers, "…news for you."

I sank into the plastic chair in front of the Coach's desk and sucked in the sweat-stained air of the gym. The place was so familiar it was like a second home. Hard to believe I'd be leaving forever in less than six months. "About what, Coach?"

He peered at me over a nose that had been broken more than once. "Your college football career, of course."

A chill raced through my body as my heart started pounding in my chest.

"I've received two more letters of commitment for you, son." He slapped his hand down on the desk. "It's your pick, Kellen. You're the most-recruited athlete we've ever had at Griffin, even after your injury. Those training films we made last week paid off. The scouts could see that you were as strong as ever."

He pulled two letters from the pile of junk on his desk and held them out for me to take. "From Stanford and Oregon State University. Take these home and talk it over with your parents. Tell them to call me if they want to discuss any of these offers."

Coach stood up and stuck out his hand. "It's been an honor to coach you, Kellen. You're an exceptional athlete with a very bright future ahead of you. Play it smart, son, and you've got it made. You can go to the college of your choice."

I shook the coach's hand and accepted the letters. "Thank you, sir. It's been an honor to have you coach me."

"Aw, get out of here." He looked embarrassed but pleased at the same time. "Go celebrate, kid."

I looked at the letters as I exited the room. Both had a fancy letterhead with a building etched on the top by the name of the school. They were all addressed to Mr. Kellen Peterson, care of Coach Branson, Griffin High School. I carefully folded them and slipped them inside my jacket.

MY NEW FIFTH period class was an AP English Lit class. I'd missed the entire first semester but the teacher had okayed for me to start second semester as they had started a new curriculum. I walked in seconds before the bell rang. I glanced around as I headed for the back of the room and my eyes riveted on a familiar dark head. My heart skipped a beat. Ivy was in this class?

I slid into one of the two vacant seats in the back row trying to decide how I felt about that. Just as the bell rang, Laurel rushed in the door. She was wearing her cheerleader outfit for a basketball game tonight and her long legs were lean and tan—even in January.

"Sorry, Mr. Pitman," she called out as she rushed to her seat, as if she and the teacher were best buds. She slid into the desk next to mine. "Hi," she whispered at me. "What a surprise." There was a grin on her face that made me think that somehow she already knew I was in this class.

Chapter Forty-Seven

Ivy

I'd heard the gossip before I got to fifth period. It was all over school that Q and Laurel had gotten back together. I tried to convince myself I was happy for him, but it felt like I'd swallowed a chicken head. And there was nothing holy about that.

"It can't be true," Mira whispered when we were at the locker. She had a perplexed look on her face.

I pulled my heavy trig book off the shelf. "I think he really liked her, Mira." It was true, even though it practically killed me to say the words. "I saw his face last fall when she came into the classroom to deliver a note to the teacher. He was like a love-sick puppy."

Mira made her vampire noise in the back of her throat. "But she dumped him when he needed her most."

The words rang with a damning resonance. So had I. "Apparently, he forgave her." I tugged on Mira's arm. "C'mon, let's go. I'm sick of talking about Q anyway."

I WAS SITTING in fifth period counting the minutes until I could escape from school. Today had been the longest day of my life. I just wanted to get away from Griffin High and not think about any of it anymore. Not Q. Not Laurel. Not true love. What? Why did I think that? I wanted to think about college—and the glorious, exciting future I was going to have somewhere far away from here.

I was drawing wings in the margins of my notebook as I waited for class to start. Just as the bell rang someone breezed in the door and sang out 'sorry!' in a way that didn't sound like they were sorry at all. I looked up in disbelief. Laurel Simmons was in this class?

My gaze followed her as she hurried to the back of the room to find a vacant chair. She was very pretty. In a blond, cheerleader sort of way. A pair of broad shoulders caught my eye. He had his head turned toward Laurel to say something to her but I'd recognize those sun-kissed locks of hair anywhere. The chicken head in my stomach squawked. Both Laurel and Q were in this class?

Chapter Forty-Eight

Kellen

"Hey Ivy, wait up." I hurried through the crowded hallway trying to catch up with her. She'd bolted from class like a cat in front of a hose. I slid up next to her and readjusted my backpack over my shoulder. "That's funny we have fifth period together still, isn't it?"

"Yeah." She gave me a weird look. "Funny." She kept walking. I wondered if she'd heard about Laurel.

I dodged a few people in the hallway. "What class do you have now?"

I swore she blushed. "I still have study hall. With Mira. Same as always."

I didn't tell her that I had study hall still, too. When I'd changed my schedule I couldn't bring myself to totally remove every chance I'd have to see her. I'd decided if I couldn't handle being around her, I'd just leave.

She glanced up at me then looked away fast. "How did your classes go today? You know…."

"Without my tutor?"

She was wearing a tight jade green sweater with a scoop neck and a carved jade necklace. I could see black lace peeking out from the neckline of her sweater. Elegant was a word that described her perfectly. As well as lovely.

"Yeah." She threaded her long hair behind her ear, looking guilty. "Without your tutor."

"Fine." I slid my hand under her elbow and pulled her toward the double doors of the library. I grabbed one of the heavy blue doors and yanked it open as I tipped my head toward the room. "Can you come in for a minute and talk?"

"Uh…okay."

I led her around the tables to a back corner where we could have some privacy. Though the bookcases were short, big plants overflowed on top of them, creating visual walls. I pulled out a chair for her to sit on, then sat across from her.

"You were right, Ivy. I'm ready to handle school on my own again. It was time for me to get back to normal." If I wanted to do this right—we had to go back to being friends first. "I want you to know that I understand why you quit tutoring me and it's okay. But I couldn't have done it without your help. I'd never have been able to maintain my grades and get caught up again if it weren't for you—so I'm really grateful for that."

Her shoulders sagged with relief. "I was glad to help, Q."

There was a bit of an awkward silence as I tried to figure out what to say next. "How was your break?"

"*Long.*" She said it with such emphasis that I smiled. Maybe she'd wanted that break to end as badly as I had. "How was yours?"

"Long." We both laughed.

"Listen— "

"Listen— "

We stopped and laughed again. Then she kept talking, which wasn't like Ivy at all.

"Q, I'm sorry things worked out the way they did. You know—all of it." She seemed like she wanted to say more, so I waited. Instead she looked at her hands, rubbing her thumb over fingers. Finally she just said, "I'm really sorry."

"It's all right, Ivy." I was trying to being super-cool, even though I ached with all the things I wanted to say. "I'm glad we're friends. That's what's most important right now."

She nodded. "Thanks." She searched my face and I swear there was something there…something that looked like what I was feeling. "Well," she stood up. "I better get going."

"Wait." I wrapped my hand around her wrist, my fingers easily circling her thin arm. "Before you go—I…I was wondering if I could talk to you about something."

Chapter Forty-Nine

Ivy

I sank back down, my heart pounding against my ribs. "Sure, Q, what is it?"

He brushed his hand across his forehead, his beautiful fingers smoothing his hair to the side. He still wore it long, the way I liked it.

"I need your advice."

"About what?"

"I've been offered scholarships to several colleges to play football, but—" he braced his elbows on his knees and looked down at his hands as if struggling to complete his sentence.

"But what?"

"My doctor and my mom—" he hesitated, a pained expression crossed his face— "*and* my sister, don't want me to play football again. Ever." He sighed as he dropped his head to run his fingers through his hair. When he looked up again I could see the anguish in his eyes. "I don't know what to do, Ivy."

Just like that—I could see the young man behind the curtain again. Q was being totally open and honest, so different from the star quarterback that everybody else saw. My heart zinged. Why, oh why did he do this to me?

"We're a lot alike, Ivy. We put the same kind of pressure on ourselves—have the same need to succeed. What do you think I should do?"

I was flattered and surprised that he'd want my opinion, but at the same time, it was a dangerous question. Q had grown up dreaming of being a football star. Did he really want me to tell him I didn't want him to play? That I thought football was a stupid and brutal sport?

He must have sensed my hesitation. "Just tell me the truth, Ivy. Tell me what you honestly think."

I owed him the truth. I took a deep breath. "I know how much you love football, Q. I know how much you love the game—how good you are." I wanted to reach out and touch him, to reassure him, but I didn't. Touching turned to craving with Q and I couldn't go there again.

I tried to keep my voice level, to not let any of my emotions seep in, but it was hard. "You're more than just an athlete. You're special, Q. I can see it in the way the other kids look up to you, in how the teachers respect you." I hesitated.

"But?"

My voice softened and I couldn't help myself—I put my hand on his arm. His skin warmed my fingertips and I didn't want to let go. "The truth is, I don't want you to play football either. I don't want you to ever be hurt again. Football is a brutal sport. If you keep playing—eventually you'll get hurt again. It's inevitable." I pulled my hand away. "I'm sorry, I know that's probably not what you wanted to hear."

He pushed himself upright and stood up. His face was perfectly blank and I had no idea what he was thinking. "Thanks for being honest, Ivy."

Q walked me to study hall and then left. I watched him through the big glass windows, his shoulders hunched as though he was carrying a heavy load, his head down, staring at his feet as he walked.

A pang of longing pierced my heart. I missed hanging out with Q and Mira. "I wish we could all just be friends again," I whispered.

Chapter Fifty

Kellen

For the first time in my life I was confused about what I wanted to do after high school. Not only was I confused about what I wanted to do, but about everything else that I'd always taken for granted.

I skipped sixth period and headed home. I flopped on my bed and scrunched the pillow behind my head as I stared up at the ceiling. I had five offers from Pac-12 college teams. It was my dream come true. All those years of hard work had paid off, even after my brain injury. But now I wasn't sure if it was the right decision.

Logically, the answer was simple. Why take a chance of messing with my brain again? God knows I didn't ever want to go through a repeat of these last three months.

But emotionally, the equation was different. Who would I be if I didn't play football? What happened to the dream I'd held almost all my life? Would people still like me if I wasn't the star quarterback? Would *I* like me?

My stomach twisted with indecision. In the past, I'd toyed with the idea of being a doctor, before football became the obvious choice. Now, nothing was obvious.

I grabbed my basketball and tossed it in the air over my head, the orange leather and black lines swirling into a blur, before I caught it again. Ivy wanted to go to Harvard. It was hard to admit it to myself, but part of me wanted to go where Ivy went. I didn't want to lose her yet. It was the first time I'd ever met somebody who was so much like me. Someone who felt right for me.

Disgusted, I pushed myself off the bed and grabbed my basketball. I couldn't make my plans based on somebody else's dreams. I had to follow my own dreams. I headed downstairs and out to our driveway. Maybe the cold air and shooting some hoops would clear my head. It was crazy to be thinking like this.

But an hour later, instead of clearing my head, I'd come up with a crazy idea.

Chapter Fifty-One

Ivy

A week after Q dragged me into the library and asked me what I thought he should do, he signed with Stanford University. Ollie Walker and Charlie Jackson both signed with the University of Washington. The local papers interviewed all of them and ran it as front page news. Even the Seattle TV stations carried the story.

I was shocked by Q's decision. With so many people he cared about telling him not to play, I kind of thought he wouldn't. But now, I could see how silly that was. A full ride to Stanford was nothing to walk away from. It was a difficult school to get into *any* time, and especially if you didn't have a legacy connection—someone in your family who had attended. But playing Pac-12 ball had been Q's dream and he'd earned it—why would I expect him to give up on it? Hopefully, he'd enjoy every second of his time at Stanford. And stay healthy.

Though I tried not to think about it, the reality of our changing futures was never far from my mind. With Q going to California and the possibility that I might attend school on the east coast—I wondered if I would ever see him again after we graduated.

KELLEN WAS AT school the next day, but you could hardly get near him for the crush of kids wanting to congratulate him. Or just touch him. He was so adored. I spotted Laurel's blond head in the group surrounding him.

"It's almost like we never really even knew him, isn't it?" Mira said, as we stood at the other end of the hall and watched. "It's like the beginning of school again."

I slammed my locker shut, the metal door clanging. "You're the one who said he wouldn't hang out with us once he didn't need us." I looped my arm through hers and turned her to go out the back door so we could avoid the crush. "Be glad he's well. We saved him, just like you wanted. Now it's time to move on."

"Yeah," Mira said softly. "You're right. But—"

"But nothing." I put both hands on her back and shoved her out the door.

I glanced over my shoulder as I went out the door. Q was moving in the opposite direction down the hall, his back to me, still surrounded. I could hear him laugh about something and then to my surprise, he turned back and looked straight at me, almost like he knew I was there.

LIKE NORMAL, I checked the mailbox after Mira dropped me off at home. Usually, there was only the normal pile of bills and flyers, but today there was a cream colored envelope with the word VE RI TAS spelled out on what looked like three open books over a maroon shield. The black letters next to the shield read **HARVARD UNIVERSITY**. My hands started to shake.

I slid my finger under the corner edge and sliced the envelope open. The letter seemed to magically unfold in my hands.

'We are honored to inform you of your acceptance into…'

Tears filled my eyes. All of my hard work was paying off. My dreams—and my parent's dreams—were coming true. But how was I supposed to feel when the dream of college took me away from a dream of true love?

Chapter Fifty-Two

Kellen

Two days after I signed with Stanford my mom said, "I've made an appointment in Seattle. I need you to drive me." I hadn't discussed my decision to sign with Stanford with either my mom or my dad. I'd turned eighteen in January and decided I wasn't going to argue with them. I was going to have one sure plan for my life after high school.

I looked up in surprise. I was sitting at the kitchen table eating a peanut butter and jelly sandwich and reading the article about me, CJ and Ollie signing, as well as some other players in town. "What's the appointment for?"

"I need to visit a lab. You know I don't like to drive in the city traffic." She picked up a stack of magazines and headed for the family room. "It won't take long. We'll leave after school tomorrow."

SINCE WHEN DID my mom not like to drive in Seattle traffic? She went into the city all the time, even though the roads were very congested and half the time the freeway was total gridlock. I drove her Volvo sedan as she directed me to a big facility on Eastlake Avenue across the street from Lake Union.

"What are you picking up?" I asked again as I parked the car. "Should I wait here?"

"No, I need you to come with me." She slid out the door and tightened the belt on her black coat. She hadn't talked much on the ride over and part of me was getting scared. What the heck was going on? Did my mom have cancer or something?

"Is everything okay, Mom?" I looked at the side of her face as we walked in the big glass entry doors. "You're not, like, *sick* or anything, are you?" My palms were a little sweaty and I wiped them on the sides of my jeans.

"I'm fine. Don't worry." She led me to the elevator bank like she knew where she was going. We exited on the fifth floor and mom led me down a hallway to a doorway on the left. A small sign on it said 'Laboratory Three'. She knocked twice, then poked her head in the door. "Dr. Anton?"

There was a muffled reply and my mom pushed the door open and walked in. It was like walking into a stainless steel surgical center. Long shining silver tables stretched across the room with cabinets and counters on each side.

A petite woman, with dark hair wearing a white doctor's jacket approached us with her hand out.

"Hello Jane. So nice to see you again." She looked at me. "And this must be Kellen."

"Yes." My mom motioned at me. "This is my son, Kellen. Kellen, this is Dr. Anton." I smiled and shook the doctor's hand, wondering what in the hell was going on. "She's a neurological researcher. Her particular area of study is brains."

Warning bells started going off in my head.

"Dr. Anton has received a donation recently. A dozen brains from deceased NFL, college and high school football players." My mother's voice shifted ever so slightly. "I wanted you to see for yourself what they looked like."

My emotions warred between utter disbelief and utter pissed-off-ness. I swiveled my head. "Seriously, Mom?"

"Come this way, Kellen. I've got the brains on this table over here." Dr. Anton walked across the room and I followed her while I widened my eyes with a WTF? look at my mom. She got my message. And totally ignored it.

"These are the brains of CTE victims," Dr. Anton said, waving her hand at an array of slides with brown tissue slices attached. The slides were surrounded by a row of white plastic containers. I glanced in a few and sure as shit, there were brown clumps of tissue that looked just like half of someone's brain.

"CTE?" I slid my hands into my pockets so I wouldn't touch anything and looked at the slides with a mixture of morbid fascination and disgust. Wasn't that what Dr. Murdoch had mentioned too?

"Chronic Traumatic Encephalopathy," Dr. Anton said in a matter-of-fact voice. "It's also known as dementia pugilistica or punch-drunk syndrome because in the past, the overwhelming majority of its victims were boxers." She picked up a sleeve of slides and held them up to the light. "But not anymore."

After she positioned the slide she swung her head over to look at me. "A disturbing trend has been discovered between CTE and high impact sports such as hockey, soccer and

238

especially football." She motioned to a microscope on the table. "Take a look."

I leaned down and gazed through the eye holes.

"What you're looking at is a normal brain."

I could see clear, pinkish-grey tissue. Hard to believe that was a slice of someone's brain. "And this— " she swapped out the slide for a new one. The new section was covered with brown spots. "— is a brain with CTE. All those brown spots are tau, which is a protein that is released when the brain suffers some kind of trauma."

My stomach clenched, like I was doing crunches. Looking at those two samples reminded me of the endless drug lectures they'd drilled into our heads during health class: here's your brain, and here's your brain on football.

"What does CTE do to you?" I stared at the speckled, gross slide. The difference between the two samples was startling. And disturbing.

"Common symptoms of CTE include memory loss, paranoia and depression in middle age. There is a possibility that several recent suicides of athletes are linked to CTE, as well." She shifted another slide under the lens. "Some athletes have even donated their brains to CTE research upon their deaths. The links are irrefutable, but we are just beginning to realize the far-reaching implications and causes of this disease."

I straightened up, suddenly sick to my stomach. "How do you get it?"

"Brain trauma. There is a link between high contact sports, like football," she tipped her head at me, "and the occurrence of CTE. It seems that today's football helmets are actually increasing the problem—because they've become more like battering rams for the players than protection.

"But don't the helmets protect their heads?"

"Ah." She held her gloved hand up. "A common misconception. While the helmets protect the outside of the head—the problem occurs when the soft brain tissue inside slams into the cranium—that's what causes the damage."

The doctor motioned to the slides spread out across the table. "Football players suffer 43,000 to 67,000 concussions per year and estimates suggest that 50% go unreported. We're now finding that players experiencing subconcussive blows—without ever reporting an actual concussion—are suffering this same sort of brain damage."

My stomach did a slow roll.

"Alzheimer's, depression and other memory-related diseases are inevitable with this kind of injury." She looked up at me. "Do you have any questions?"

I took a step back and looked at my mom. She was waiting behind me—letting me get my fill. "No, doc. I think I've seen enough."

MOM AND I didn't talk for half of the ride home. I was still trying to wrap my head around everything I'd just seen and learned. Did I have tau protein gumming up my brain right now?

"I thought it was important that you know the facts, Kellen." Mom's voice was perfectly neutral. "Your father and I have encouraged you to play football all these years, never realizing the danger we were putting you in. When I saw you in that hospital bed, unable to move— " her tough veneer cracked— "all over a stupid *game*. I will *never* willingly let you play football again. I can't allow you to put yourself in harm's way for *nothing*."

I reached over and patted her shoulder. "Thanks Mom. I guess maybe I should tell you about plan B."

Chapter Fifty-Three

Ivy

The next few weeks passed in a blur. It was already the middle of March and next weekend was Tolo – the formal dance where girls asked boys to attend. Then the next week was spring break and the orchestra group was headed to Paris. I couldn't wait to escape.

Brandon was going out with Jenny McNamara again. Tank and Mira broke up, but ever since coming to her rescue at The Crypt, Charlie Jackson had been hanging around her a lot more. Q was his normal friendly self, just like nothing had ever happened between us. When I'd wished that we could all be friends again, I should have been more careful with what I'd wished.

Apparently, Q still had sixth period study hall, because he'd show up there three or four days a week, but he never sat with me and Mira. He was always surrounded by other people, usually half were girls drooling over him. I'd catch him looking our way occasionally, and he'd wave from across the room if our eyes met, but he never made any attempt to talk.

"He's kind of like the sun, isn't he?" Mira mused one day as she licked the cream from the center of a Twinkie. "It's like half the students in the school orbit him."

"Yeah, it's the gravitational pull—like flies and shit."

Mira turned to look at me, her brows pulled down in a frown. "Are you okay?"

"Just stating the facts, M'am." I didn't look up from the science write-up I was working on. It hurt too much. I ached with missing him. Missing what I could have had with him. At night, I'd lay in the dark, my arms clutched around my pillow and remember our conversations, his expressions, the feel of his hands on my face, in my hair. I had Ivy's Song memorized and the hauntingly beautiful notes would play in my head as I pictured him sitting at that piano, playing for me. I swear it would have been better to never have loved him, then to love him like this and never have him.

Mira shrugged. "Okay, whatever." She licked her fingers, the Twinkie consumed. "Are you going to ask anyone to Tolo?"

I snorted out a laugh. "Like who?"

Mira shrugged. "I don't know." She looked across the room. "Maybe you should ask Q."

I narrowed my eyes at her. Was this a test of some kind? We'd never actually talked about me dating Q. Mira had only acknowledged that he wasn't interested in her. "What?"

Mira squirmed in her seat. "It was just an idea." She was dressed like an anime character today, with the spiky bangs hanging over her eyes and her hair in two ponytails on each side. She wore a black choker around her neck and a black jacket with some sort of sexy lace-up corset thing underneath.

I'm not sure if she was supposed to be a vampire or a vampire hunter, but her fingernails were painted blood red along with her lips. "You could ask Q and I could ask CJ."

My mouth dropped open. "*What?*"

"You heard me," she said in a defensive tone. "It'd be fun."

There were so many thoughts racing through my head that I honestly couldn't think of a response. Finally, I croaked, "but I thought you were in love with Q?"

Mira shrugged, looking slightly guilty. "He's not really my type." She bent her fingers and examined her nails. "A little too goal-oriented for me." She looked up and smiled brightly. "But CJ's fun."

A ray of hope burst through me. Was Mira telling me it was okay for me to like Q?

Someone shouted at the far end of the room, drawing our attention. As we watched Kendra Brown ran up to Mrs. Monoghan, the study hall teacher, waving her arms. After a brief conversation, the teacher turned and followed the girl out of the room.

"Wonder what that was all about?" I asked.

A minute later the doors to the study hall room burst open. Laurel came marching in wearing a black trench coat, followed by two guys carrying trumpets.

"Oh, this can't be good," Mira murmured.

Laurel waltzed over to where Q was sitting with a bunch of guys and hopped on the table in front of him. As soon as her feet landed, the band starting playing 'the Stripper."

Mira hissed in the back of her throat. "Oh. My. God."

Every head in study hall turned to watch.

Laurel swung her hips in time to the music and flung off her trench coat. Somebody hooted and a few cat calls joined in. Q sat with his arms crossed over his chest, a grin on his face as he watched.

"Why doesn't he walk away?" Mira snapped. "He must be mortified."

He didn't look mortified, but I was. How could I have even let myself think I had a chance with him? "He looks like he's enjoying it to me," I said. And he did.

Piece by piece Laurel's garments went flying as she twisted and gyrated to the music. The guys in the room started clapping and chanting 'take it off'. She finally peeled down to a black string bikini. She raised her hands over her head and slowly turned so everyone in the room could see her well-endowed body. 'Kellen' was written across her stomach in black ink and 'Tolo?' was written low across her back.

The clapping was a thunderous steady chant of *yes, yes, yes* as everyone waited for Q's answer.

"Ivy, did he just look at you?" Mira whispered in a shocked voice. She poked my arm. "He did. I saw him. Q just looked at you."

I ignored her. I had to see what his response would be.

Then Q nodded yes.

Chapter Fifty-Four

Kellen

Coach continued to work with me on my exercise routines. "Gotta keep you in shape, Kellen. Those college coaches want you to hit the ground running." I didn't mind. These were no-contact work-outs, with a lot of passing, running drills, hand and foot precision work, which was all good to rebuild and fine-tune the coordination on my right side. Plus, it gave me something to think about besides Ivy.

After I'd come up with my crazy idea I'd started the wheels in motion but I hadn't heard anything back yet. The more time that passed, the more I thought about Dr. Anton and her brains, the more sure I became that maybe my idea wasn't that crazy after all.

I WENT TO sixth period study hall almost every day just so I could see Ivy. But it was a hopeless cause. She made no attempt to talk to me and barely looked at me most of the time. I'd heard she'd been accepted at Harvard. She already felt so far away and out of reach. I tried to convince myself that I didn't care about her. I was sure I'd stop thinking about her soon. I had to—because I was driving myself crazy.

TOLO WAS THE third weekend of March. It was a girl-ask-boy formal event. Laurel and I had gone last year but I figured this year I just wouldn't go. I'd purposely kept things cool between us, but when she'd stripped and asked me to the dance, I'd thought 'what the hell?'

Chapter Fifty-Five

Ivy

For a moment after Q nodded his head, I thought I was going to throw up.

"You've got to be kidding me," Mira hissed.

Laurel launched herself into his arms. I sat frozen, staring at them.

"He'll regret that," Mira snarled. "Mark my words."

I jerked back around and stared blindly at my science notes. I wanted to leave but I didn't want to reveal how upset I was—not to Mira or Q. Tears boiled up behind my eyes and I knew I couldn't sit there any longer without completely humiliating myself. I slammed my science notebook shut and shoved it into my backpack.

"I've gotta go." I didn't look at Mira, or Q, or anyone as I bolted from the room. I just stared at the floor, intent on escaping.

"Ivy!" Mira called after me. I slammed my way out through the metal exterior door. The bar to open the door

247

sounded like an explosion when I hit it. As soon as I was outside I ran for it. Tears streamed down my face. I couldn't allow anyone, not even Mira, to see me like this. I ran the other direction from where we parked Jefferson and cut through the side parking lot. My eyes flooded with tears, making it hard to see. My nose was running and my breath was coming out in hiccupping gasps. I swiped at my face and my hand came away smeared with black mascara.

I dodged between a red Mustang and a black Nissan. As I passed, a face looked up at me from the driver's side of the Nissan. Ollie Walker's eyes got as wide as two pancakes as I ran by. That just made me cry harder. Behind me, I heard his door open.

"Hey, you okay?"

I raced across the lot without answering and pushed my way through a hedge of old trees and bushes. The other side was a tangle of residential streets. I zigged and zagged up one street and down another until I didn't even know where I was. I found a vacant lot and sat down behind on old tree on the far corner. Then I really cried.

Chapter Fifty-Six

Kellen

Ollie told me he'd seen Ivy crying. Mira called me and reamed me a new asshole. If Ivy came to school before spring break started, I didn't see her. She was leaving tomorrow morning with her orchestra group for Paris.

I told Laurel I couldn't go to Tolo and that I didn't want to date her. Not pleasant, but necessary.

I laid in bed and stared into the dark, *again*, thinking about Ivy. Tomorrow spring break started. Would I ever be able to fix this?

Chapter Fifty-Seven

Ivy

It was raining in Paris, which seemed so totally appropriate. It was our third day and our orchestra group was required to be up early to take the tour bus to see the sights. Brandon sat in the back with Jenny McNamara. They seemed happy to be back together. I couldn't believe how much I missed Mira. I wouldn't allow myself to think about Q.

Raindrops pounded the windows, streaking down the pane like tears, distorting the view. The sky was low and grey, pressing down. At the front of the bus, the windshield wipers slapped back and forth, trying to keep up with the torrent that drenched the city.

The traffic was thick as we drove around the Arc de Triomphe, our tour bus giving us an elevated view. Around us, red taillights seemed to stretch forever. Our guide kept a running dialog in her beautifully accented English, describing the sites we were passing. I listened with half an ear, staring out at the view with a sense of disbelief that I was really, finally here. Paris. Another dream come true.

Yet, there was an emptiness eating a hole in my stomach. We crossed a bridge and the guide announced that the Eiffel Tower was on the left. I turned to look and there it was. Just like in all the pictures. Iconic and magnificent, stretching into the grey mist above.

The kids on the bus started whooping in excitement and I pressed my nose against the cold window. Mira would love it if she were here – rain or no rain. I smiled. Knowing Mira, she would probably like it better *with* the rain—so quintessentially Paris.

Quintessentially. Q. Don't think of Q words, I admonished myself. Don't think of Q. But I couldn't seem to think of anything else.

We drove right underneath the Eiffel Tower before we stopped to unload. There was a lot of excited chatter as the kids crowded into the aisle to exit. I waited patiently in my seat for the glut of kids to pass.

"Ivy." Brandon nudged me as he was going by. "Get up— we're here!" He was holding Jenny's hand and smiled over his shoulder at her as he made space for me. "We're in Paris!"

My heart pinged as I forced a smile and stood up. "Thanks."

The rain continued to pour down but street vendors miraculously appeared selling umbrellas for five dollars American.

As our teacher tried to get us to queue up, I stared in awe at the beautifully intricate grid work of the Eiffel Tower. It soared above our heads like an elegant sentinel from the past. So much more magnificent in real life than the display they'd had at Homecoming.

Mr. Flynn was leading the group toward a rickety old elevator, circa sometime in the last century, to take us up to the restaurant. I was at the back of the line, trying to delay risking my life in that tiny box. I surveyed the crowd of kids to see if anyone else seemed worried about being trapped amid the antiquity when a pair of shoulders caught my eye. That looked like—

My heart skipped a beat before I caught myself. Of course it wasn't. Those shoulders couldn't possibly belong to Q. I was in Paris.

France.

Far, far from home.

For just a moment I gave in and allowed myself to stare longingly at the young man's back, letting myself imagine that Q was here with me. He turned.

Wait a minute.

My heart stopped.

He was smiling with a crazy-cute dimple on one side.

"Bonjour Ivy." Q walked toward me as if he hung out under the Eiffel Tower every day. There was no limp, no weird lip thing, no curled right hand. He walked with the confidence and swagger of a star quarterback. He was as beautiful as any boy could ever be. He stopped before me and reached for my hands. "I couldn't let you come to Paris without me. Don't you know it's the City of Love?"

I couldn't think of a single coherent thing to say. Not even to correct him to say it was known as the City of Light. I liked love much better.

"Q! W..What are you doing here?" I finally stuttered.

"Didn't I ever tell you?" That damn dimple winked at me and his eyes had a suspicious glint like he was laughing inside. "My sister studies music at the University of Paris. Our family has been planning this trip since last fall."

He reached up to swing around a messenger bag he carried on his shoulder, looking very European. "I've got something for you." He lifted the flap and dug into the interior. "Well, actually, Mira sent it." I gasped as he pulled out the iridescent purple wrap from my Homecoming gown. The one part of my outfit that hadn't been puked on. The fabric sparkled like a million diamonds had been stitched on its surface.

"She said you'd need this." He straightened the shawl and the beautiful fabric sparkled in the—sunshine? I glanced up and sure enough, there was a shaft of light pouring through a parting in the clouds, like light shining down from heaven. Q swung the gauzy wrap around my shoulders, his fingers lingering. "Mira was mumbling something about Cinderella when she gave it to me— " he had a confused twist to his brow— "but to tell you the truth, I couldn't really follow what she was talking about."

"Mira sent that?" I asked, hope and fear twisting a web in my throat, almost choking me.

He grinned. "Mira's known exactly how I've felt about you since Christmas break. I asked her not to tell you—I wanted to do that. I've been trying to find the right time, but…" Q reached a finger out and threaded a strand of hair out my face, his fingers gentle and warm against my skin. "It never seemed to work out. I want you to know that I didn't go to Tolo with Laurel. We never got back together and I've made it clear to her that I'm in love with someone else."

I covered my mouth with shaking fingers.

His blue eyes looked deep into mine. "I love you, Ivy. More than I've ever loved anyone in my life."

"You do?" I sounded pathetic. And I didn't even care.

His voice softened. "I don't want to lose you. Not now, not next fall, not ever."

"But you're going to Stanford, and— " a bit of my happiness shriveled. I practically whispered the words— "I've been accepted at Harvard."

"I know. Mira told me in February." His lips had a mischievous twist to them. "I was too."

I took a step back. "Wait. What?"

"I've been accepted at Harvard, too. Their School of Engineering and Applied Sciences is doing heavy research on traumatic brain injury. They've accepted me both as an incoming freshman and as a subject in the study." He grinned at me with a perfect smile. "Stanford was Plan B. In case my real plan didn't work out."

"No more football?" I was afraid to hope.

He shook his head. "Homecoming was my last game."

"Oh Q!" I stood on tiptoe and threw my arms around his broad shoulders, squeezing as tight as I could. Dreams do come true.

He wrapped his arms around me and pulled me close, whispering in my ear, "I love you so much, Ivy."

"I love you too, Q. More than anything. " His lips parted and he kissed me. Soft and gentle, like summer fruit and cherry coke. He slid his fingers into my hair and framed my face with his big hands. I wrapped my arms around his neck, caressing the strength of his shoulders, his muscles bunching beneath my fingers. I pressed myself close to him as our kiss deepened. I loved kissing him.

"Ah, so sweet," said a voice clearly directed at us. The English was laced with a thick French accent. We both turned to look. It was a young man dressed in black trousers and a black vest covering his white shirt. His sleeves were held up by black armbands like a photographer from a different era. He had a thin moustache above his lip and a black beret covered his dark hair. "A photograph for the lovebirds?" He lifted an old-fashioned looking camera. "So you'll never forget thees happy time in Paris, the City of Love."

Click.

Chapter Fifty-Eight

Ivy

"Ivy—" Mira rolled her eyes— "it was *so* obvious. Everybody knew Q was crazy about you for months."

"You're okay with that?" We'd arrived home at two in the morning the previous night, but I was already up and over at Mira's. I couldn't wait to tell her—to make sure everything was okay.

"Of course," Mira scoffed. "He told me he loved you way back during Christmas break. That guy's got it so bad for you—I'm surprised he didn't propose in Paris."

ONE MONTH LATER we were in Mira's room again. She held her fingers out and blew on nails she'd just painted sparkling black. "It's called Midnight Elegance." She wiggled her fingers for me to see. "It goes with my dress. *Very* sophisticated."

We were going to Prom. With dates. "You're going to be a knock-out tonight," I said. And she was. Her hair was blond with just a small streak of black threaded through one section and swept to the side and pinned back behind her head with a sparkling clip. She was wearing a long, sleek black gown embellished with little sequins that sparkled like a thousand suns in the light. She was beautiful. "CJ's not going to know what hit him."

Mira grinned. "I know." She screwed the lid back on the nail polish, her fingers splayed to dry. "I have other news, too."

"Oh? What's that?"

"Ollie and Jasmine are getting married! They're going to live in Seattle and raise the baby there while Ollie plays football for the U."

"That's wonderful. It doesn't sound easy, but Ollie and Jazzy love each other. They can make it work."

"Well, if they need a babysitter, at least I'll be able to help them out." Mira had a smug look on her face.

I was busy straightening the skirt of the black gown I was wearing. "How's that?" I asked.

"I've been accepted at U-Dub, too." She grinned at me. "I'm going to college."

"Mira!" I grabbed for her hands. "That's awesome."

"Watch the nails, watch the nails," she cried, holding her hands out of my reach, but her lips twitched in a grin.

"What will you study?"

She shrugged. "My dad has mentioned something about an internship after I get my degree but I think I'm meant for the stage." She struck a pose and grinned at me.

"Of course you are. And how handy that CJ is going to be going to school there, too."

She waggled her eyebrows at me. "I know. Just like you and Q at Harvard." Mira blew on her nails. "Have you given up on your dream to live in Paris?"

My answer came from my heart. "I've been to Paris with the boy I love. I don't need to live there anymore. Besides, who knows? Maybe the four of us will be exchange students some day." I nudged her knee and grinned at her. "Remember, life is all about choices—*anything* is possible."

Chapter Fifty-Nine

Kellen

Ivy and I danced with the rest of the seniors beneath the sparkling chandelier in the grand ballroom where prom was being held. Reflections of snowflakes twirled around on the ceiling as if they were falling from the sky. The whole effect was magical.

The music changed to a slow song and I held my arms out to Ivy. She slid into my embrace like I was made to hold her. I rested my cheek against her silky hair as we rocked slowly to the music.

Nine months ago I thought my life had ended. Now, I felt like I had endless possibilities. I put my finger under Ivy's chin and tilted her face up to mine so I could kiss her. I guess Homecoming wasn't my last dance after all.

Author's Note

Though THE LAST DANCE is a work of fiction, the type of traumatic brain injury that Kellen suffers is very real. Chronic Traumatic Encephalopathy, or CTE, is a disease resulting from trauma to the brain. Researchers have found a disturbing association between CTE and football injuries.

The recent suicides of professional football players, Junior Seau, Ray Easterling and Dave Duerson have forced a rising tide of concern regarding traumatic brain injuries and their link to football. No other contact sport gives rise to as many serious injuries. Studies are showing that players who are receiving sub-concussive blows are just as much at risk as those who have been diagnosed with concussion.

The program that Q was accepted into, Harvard's School of Engineering and Applied Sciences (SEAS) really exists and is "using cutting-edge tissue engineering techniques—essentially creating a living brain on a chip—biologists, physicists, engineers, and materials scientists have been collaborating on the study of brain injury and potential targets for treatment."

***

"Where words fail, music speaks," wrote Danish author Hans Christian Andersen. But researchers are learning that music may also encourage speech in patients suffering the debilitating effects of strokes and other neurological conditions.

"We are just beginning to understand the immense potential of music to enhance lives, improve health and increase our understanding of the human brain," says Music Education Professor Steven M. Demorest, conference organizer. "While ICMPC has been meeting since 1989, there has been an explosion of research in this area in the last decade or so. Even with this increasing activity, the study of music perception and cognition is a relatively new field compared to research in areas such as language or visual perception. There are new findings all the time regarding how music shapes the developing brain and how musical thought and behavior relate to cognition in other domains."

Thank you for reading THE LAST DANCE.

Kiki Hamilton
April 23, 2012

Acknowledgements

Thanks to the wise words and encouragement of early readers Carly Hamilton, Jean Martin, Paula MacLaughlin and Amy Dominy.

Also, to the wonderful bloggers, librarians, booksellers and readers who have supported me in this writing journey and were willing to take a chance on a different kind of story from me – Thank you!

About the Author

Kiki Hamilton is the author of THE FAERIE RING fantasy series. She believes in magic and the idea of hidden worlds co-existing with our own. Kiki lives near Seattle, though she dreams of living in London one day. Visit her website at: www.kikihamilton.com

Made in the USA
San Bernardino, CA
10 March 2013